The Last English Village

English Village

James Ignizio

The Last English Village by James Ignizio
Cowan Creek Press

This book is a work of fiction. Names, characters, places, and incidents either are products of the author's imagination or are used fictitiously. Any resemblance to actual events or locales or persons living or dead is entirely coincidental.

Marmite is a registered trademark of Unilever PLC. All other trademarks are the property of their respective owners.

Cover Photograph: St. Mary's Church, Lower Slaughter, England. Photograph by James Ignizio. Used with permission.

ISBN-10: 1477674918
ISBN-13: 978-1477674918

CONTENTS

1
22 DECEMBER 1943:
LOWER FRITHTHINGDEN, ENGLAND

Reginald "Reg" Johnson, Warrant Officer Class 2 of the 43rd Wessex Light Infantry Regiment, stood silent vigil outside one of the matching coal-black Rolls-Royce Phantom IIIs. The choir, housed in the village church some hundred yards away, could be clearly heard. They were singing "Away in the Manger" and doing, in Reg's opinion, a damn fine job of it.

The left rear window of the other Phantom III, the one with "the man" in it, was open. Cigar smoke drifted from the window and floated lazily upward, disappearing into the afternoon sky.

While Reg enjoyed the singing, he was baffled as to just why they had paused here on their journey back to London. The village was several miles off the main road; yet they had driven at top speed to get here, only to sit and listen to a children's choir.

Reg's eyes caught those of Captain Enfield. Enfield shrugged his narrow shoulders. He too had no idea as to the reason for the unusual stopover.

It was then that Reg thought he heard the distant sound of one or more aeroplanes. If he was not mistaken, the all too familiar hum to the northeast was that of a German bomber, a twin-engine Ju88. However, the sound was rapidly diminishing. The aeroplane was evidently heading east, away from the English coastline, so he said nothing.

A moment later Reg's keen hearing picked up the sound of yet another aeroplane; this one headed in the general direction of the village. It was a four-engine craft, from the sound of it one of the Yank's big B17s, a "Flying Fortress."

Just as the choir began the first chorus of "Hark the Herald Angels Sing," Reg happened to look skyward. The thick cloud cover that had enveloped the countryside that day had broken and a beam of brilliant sunlight illuminated the nearby church. But Reg's interest was drawn to an object, drifting slowly downward from the sky.

"Sir, look there," said Reg, pointing skyward. "That looks like a parachute. What do you make of it?"

"Bloody hell," exclaimed Captain Enfield, "that parachute is connected to a German mine. God help us; I do believe it's headed for the church."

Reg and the Captain simultaneously yelled out warnings to the occupants of the Phantom IIIs. By then the parachute bomb was floating no more than five hundred feet above the church. By then it was – to all appearances – too late to do anything.

#####

Although twelve-year-old Tommy Hawkes's headache and fever had finally started to fade, his boredom grew worse by the minute. With nothing else to do and nowhere else to go, he continued what he had been doing for at least two hours: counting the birds that covered the wallpaper of his bedroom.

While tallying the number of bluebirds on the border, he was distracted by the clanking noises of the dishes his mother was washing. She tunelessly hummed "Silent Night," over and over again … and it was driving him mad! It was bad enough to be sick, bad enough to miss the Christmas play, but now he had to endure his mother's off-key humming. Although he dearly loved his mum, her inability to carry a tune was legendary in and around Lower Friththingden.

Without warning, Tommy's bed – along with the two-hundred-year-old solid brick farmhouse – shook violently. Two windowpanes in his room cracked and a third splintered, scattering shards of glass across the wooden floor. Almost simultaneously, the sound of an enormous explosion, coming from the direction of the village, shattered the quiet of the winter afternoon.

Downstairs Tommy's mother let out a shriek, which was followed by the unmistakable sound of dishes breaking. Shaking with fright, Tommy raised himself to a sitting position. As he looked out his bedroom window, a dark shadow sailed directly over the house. The young boy watched in a mix of horror and fascination as a large aeroplane pancaked to an abrupt landing in the pasture behind the house.

Although he was certain it would explode, the only upshot of the landing was a huge cloud of dust – followed by the sounds of the craft breaking in half. At first Tommy thought it must be a downed German bomber, but, as the dust settled, he was able to make out the markings on the broken fuselage. It was an American aircraft, one of their B17s, the famous Flying Fortress he had read so much about.

"Tommy," his mother cried from downstairs, "don't you dare move from that bed! I'll take care of matters." With that, he heard the kitchen door swing open and, a second later, slam shut.

Returning his gaze to the battered aircraft, Tommy watched as five men slowly emerged from the wreckage. Four of them looked dazed but none the worse for wear. The fifth, the tallest of the group, had a white bandage wrapped about his skull, almost completely covering the bloodied left side of his head.

The injured man stumbled and almost fell, dropping something from his right hand. He immediately went to his knees, frantically pawing the grass around him, trying to find whatever it was he had dropped. Two of the other crewmembers grabbed him by his arms and pulled him, protesting, to his feet.

Tommy studied the downed bomber, wondering where the rest of the crew were. He was almost certain that a B17 carried a crew of ten. But there was no movement from within the aeroplane, and none of the survivors seemed inclined to return to the wreckage. There were, he guessed, either five bodies in the fuselage or else the other crewmembers had bailed out. He prayed for the latter.

Tommy watched as his mother ran toward the men. Using every bit of energy he had, he swung his legs over the edge of the bed and reached for his prized Kodak Six-20 Folding Brownie camera on the bookcase. He was, by God, determined to get a picture of this momentous event.

The sudden movement, however, nauseated him and he had to struggle to keep from throwing up. By the time he had seized the camera and returned to the window, nothing was to be seen but the aeroplane. He heard the kitchen door open and the sounds of boots against the tile floor below.

Disappointed but undeterred, Tommy aimed the camera and took three quick snapshots of the broken aeroplane. He was ready to take a fourth when he heard yet another disconcerting sound. Two large motorcars, a matched pair of sleek black Rolls-Royce Phantom IIIs, roared into the garden behind the house – driving right through the recently painted picket fence. The car doors swung open and men streamed out of the vehicles. One group approached the plane; another headed toward the house. Most of the men were in military uniform but at least two were civilians, well dressed and important looking. Even though the civilians had their backs to him, Tommy thought that there was something very familiar about the shorter, stocky man.

Tommy raised his camera once again and took two more pictures. Exhausted by the effort, he returned the camera to its place on the bookcase and lay back down on the bed, breathing heavily – his head pounding. Downstairs he could hear the excited, muffled voices of several men speaking at once. Seconds later he fell into a troubled sleep, dreaming of aeroplanes and bluebirds falling from the sky.

2
23 DECEMBER 1943:
LOWER FRITHTHINGDEN, ENGLAND

"Tommy, are you awake?" Tommy stirred, opened his eyes and saw his mother standing over him. The light from the late morning sun filled the small room.

"Yes, Mum," he answered, wondering what her reaction would have been if he had said no.

"How are you feeling, luv? You've slept for near on fifteen hours straight."

"Better, Mum, much better."

"That's wonderful, I thought that nasty cold would pass soon," Tommy's mother replied, and then abruptly changed the subject. "Well, Tommy, my dear boy, we had quite the exciting afternoon and evening yesterday. Have you had a chance to look out your window?"

Suddenly Tommy remembered everything, the explosion in the village, the aeroplane falling from the sky, the swarm of men leaping from the two grand motorcars and, most of all, the tall Yank with the bandaged head.

"Mum," said Tommy, raising himself to a sitting position and pointing out the window, "I saw that aeroplane crash. But before that there was a huge explosion, and right after that the aeroplane crashed into our pasture."

Excited, Tommy's words came faster. "Mum, I saw five Yanks climb out of the wreckage; then two splendid Rolls-Royces drove right into our garden. Phantom IIIs, Mum, can you believe that? Look, you can see where they ran straight through the fence!"

A worried look came over his mother's face and she placed a reassuring hand on the boy's shoulder. "Tommy, you must have been delirious. An aeroplane certainly did crash into the pasture, as you can plainly see. But it was a German craft, and no one on it survived. The explosion you heard a moment before the crash was a German parachute mine scoring a direct hit on the *Sow and Centipede* pub – which was, praise God, empty at the time. The men in that aeroplane must have dropped that horrid device."

Pausing briefly, Tommy's mother continued, her face taking on an uncharacteristically grim and determined look. "There were no Rolls-Royces either, luv, just two military lorries – and they came to inspect the wreckage and remove the bodies."

Tommy could hardly believe his ears. Had he really been delirious? He looked out the window once more, focusing intently on the wreckage of the aeroplane. There was something wrong. The markings on the fuselage had been removed – or, more likely, painted over. There were, in fact, no markings to be seen, either Yank or Jerry. But Tommy had seen enough pictures of B17s to know that what remained in the pasture was indeed a Flying Fortress. He turned to his mother, about to reply. She, in turn, put her finger to her mouth and shushed him.

"Tommy, listen carefully to me. You did *not* see any men climb out of that wreckage. Everyone on board died in that crash. There were two military transports in the garden, and, as I said, they came and carried the bodies away. There will be a crew coming this afternoon to remove the wreckage. So you make sure to stay inside. Do you understand, son? Inside!"

Tommy swallowed hard. He found it difficult to believe his ears. Never in his life had he known his mother to tell a lie. "But Mum, I swear I saw the five Yanks – and the two grand motorcars. I swear it."

"No, child, for the last time you did *not* see any such thing. You imagined all that. Do you understand? This is very important, Tommy. You most certainly did not see any Americans, and you must *never* tell anyone that you did. *Never.* Do you understand?"

Tommy wanted to protest but thought better of it. Clearly, either he had actually been delirious or else his mother thought it extraordinarily important that he hadn't seen five live Americans. "I understand, Mum," he replied, not understanding at all.

After dressing, Tommy trod, a bit unsteadily, down the stair steps and into the kitchen. There he had his usual breakfast of tea, Weetabix, and fresh cream. Waiting until his mother was occupied with cleaning up the broken glass in his bedroom, Tommy quietly opened the door leading from the kitchen to the rear garden. Closing the door as softly as he could, the boy walked to the spot where he had seen, or imagined he had seen, the five airmen first appear.

Within minutes he found what he was looking for, the object the bandaged man had dropped. He bent over, took a closer look, and recoiled. It was a human ear; a blood covered human ear. Recovering his composure, Tommy took out his handkerchief and used it to pick up the ear. Wrapping the ear in the handkerchief, he raced back to the house.

That afternoon, just as his mother had promised, several lorries pulled into the back garden of the house. By nightfall the wreckage had been cleared and even the broken fence repaired. From all outward appearances, nothing out of the ordinary had ever occurred.

3
FIFTY-FOUR YEARS LATER,
18 APRIL 1997: ARRIVAL AT GATWICK

Without warning the massive Boeing 747 shuddered, rose, fell, and then – just at the moment my stomach reached my throat – leveled off. The elderly blue-haired lady next to me woke with a start and grabbed my arm, her eyes wide with fear.

"Everything's okay," I assured her, praying that I was right, "we just ran into some turbulence. Nothing to worry about." She gave me a weak smile and, visibly embarrassed, released her death grip on my arm.

"Sorry about that folks," came a reassuring voice over the intercom, "just keep those ol' seat belts fastened. It won't be long now. Gatwick has cleared us for landing and we're on our final approach. Conditions at the airport are seven degrees Celsius, overcast, with light rain. And don't forget to turn your watches ahead. Today's the 18th in England and the local time is 7:35 a.m."

I opened the window shade and peered out. The sun was up, but I could make out nothing beneath the plane but clouds. I'd have to take the pilot's word that merry old England was down there ... somewhere. If memory served me, the last time I flew into London's Gatwick airport the visibility was just as bad. That was in the spring of 1972, with Jenny seated next to me. I had thought then that would be the last time I would be forced to visit this dreary, mildewed little country. I was wrong.

It was only because of Jenny's pleas that I had agreed to that trip a quarter century ago. Ironically, it's only because of her final request that I made this one. All that I could think was that the sooner I land and get this ordeal over with, the better.

One of the few things that Jenny and I ever seriously disagreed on was England. She, for reasons beyond me, loved the country and its people. Until the onset of her illness some five years ago, she would, like clockwork, return to the land of her birth for a six-week visit each summer. I, on the other hand, found the country to be, at best, disagreeable. But, most of all, I found the people insufferable. And, most unbearable of all was Bertie, Jenny's eccentric cousin.

Bertie will supposedly be at Gatwick to greet me. At least that's what he promised me in his email. If he keeps his word this would make it the first time in roughly thirty years that the loathsome little man has ventured outside London.

Jenny positively adored Bertie, although I could never understand why. Master of the inane, non-stop disseminator of trivia, tiresome ol' Cousin Bertie was the most awful bore I had ever encountered. Given the choice between a conversation with Bertie or blowing my brains out, I'd quickly find a proper, large-caliber weapon. Given the present circumstances, however, I would have no choice but to tolerate Cousin Bertie, at least until Jenny's request was honored.

For the past thirty or so years Bertie shared a tiny two bedroom flat with his mother on London's dingy Southside. His mother, Jenny's ill-tempered aunt Fiona, was an invalid and Bertie waited on her hand and foot. At least he did until her demise from cirrhosis of the liver about nine months ago – not a surprising fate considering Aunt Fiona's thirty yearlong love affair with cheap gin.

According to Jenny, Cousin Bertie once held some lofty goals and was considered by the family to be destined for great things. But that had all changed in the split second that the car that he, his father and his mother were in was run off the road by a drunken lorry driver – somewhere on the motorway between London and Oxford.

Bertie's father died on the spot. His mother suffered a fractured hip, an injury from which she never recovered. But Bertie, who had been driving, walked away without a scratch. In retrospect he – and the world – might have been better off had he shared his father's fate.

Bertie's injuries may not have been physical, but they were there … and they were evidently permanent. He never again drove a car. He dropped out of Oxford and devoted his life to taking care of Aunt Fiona and managing the musty little news agency under their flat. Other than that his only interests seemed to be drinking warm beer, watching birds (of, sadly, the non-human variety), and studying history, particularly military history.

If you can't find Bertie in his flat, or in the neighborhood pub, or at his news agency, you need look no farther than the park across the street. Bertie spends hours at a time there watching his feathered friends – most likely his only friends. His fascination with birds is passionate to the extreme, as would anyone who attempts to feed them soon find out. Cast even a single crumb in the direction of a hungry sparrow and Bertie – shaking and red faced with anger – will rise from his bench, point a menacing finger at you and demand you leave the park. Feeding wild animals, according to Bertie, is an unspeakable evil. That sort of behavior had, not surprisingly, ultimately earned Bertie the nickname of "Birdie" amongst his neighbors.

But maybe I'm being too hard on Bertie. After all, he had agreed – almost begged – to help me find Jenny's final resting place. One thing is sure; the odd little man loved Jenny.

#####

My not so fond reminisces of Cousin Bertie were interrupted by the squeal of the landing gear striking the runway, accompanied by the braking of the engines. Once the plane arrived at the gate and the all-clear signal chimed, I hurried to retrieve my one piece of carry-on luggage from the overhead bin. The thought of anyone else touching it sickened me.

Before departing Cleveland's Hopkins airport, yesterday, I had carefully wrapped the urn containing Jenny's ashes in bubble wrap, and then placed that precious container into a stiff cardboard box. To the box I duct-taped a makeshift rope handle. Opening the luggage compartment I retrieved the carton, relieved to see that everything was intact.

After reclaiming my checked luggage, Jenny's well-travelled roll-a-board, and clearing customs, I walked through the double doors into the dim and grimy Gatwick arrivals hall. I stood there for what seemed like several minutes before finally spotting Cousin Bertie, standing at the very rear of the crowd and looking uncharacteristically somber. When our eyes met he offered me an almost indiscernible wave. To my surprise, other than for a few gray hairs, Bertie looked much the same as he had nearly twenty-five years ago. I was almost certain he was wearing the same flat tweed cap and threadbare Harris Tweed jacket he wore then.

"Lo, Vince," said Bertie, offering me his hand and giving me the customary Englishman's dead fish handshake. "How was the flight?"

"It was all right, Bertie, and how are you doing? You're certainly looking well."

"I'm doing just fine," he responded, looking questioningly at the cardboard box. "Would that be Jenny? May I give you a hand?"

My first impulse was to say no, but the forlorn look on the man's face made me change my mind. I handed the box to Bertie. For just an instant he looked as if he was going to cry, then shook his head and stiffened his upper lip. Wouldn't do, I supposed, for a proper Englishman to show emotion, and it certainly appeared that Bertie was on the verge of losing control.

"So, Bertie, how do we get to your flat? Bus? Taxi?"

"Oh no, it's much cheaper and faster to take the train to Victoria Station. In fact I've already bought your ticket, as well as my return ticket. From there we hop on the tube."

"Fine," I answered. "Lead the way."

I followed Bertie down the escalators leading to the nondescript train station beneath the airport. Waiting there was the Gatwick Express – direct service to Victoria Station. I headed toward it, thinking that it must be the train Bertie had been talking about.

"No, Vince," said Bertie, "that's the express train. We'll be taking the regular commuter train. It may not be quite as fast, but it's a lot cheaper."

Cheap, I thought, just might be Bertie's middle name. According to Jenny, and even though she thought the world of Bertie, there were rumors that he still had the first shilling he had earned.

Our train arrived at the station a few minutes later. I'd have to say that it certainly looked a lot cheaper than the express. The train, in fact, looked like it was on its last legs. My guess was that the last time it had been maintained must have been during the Boer War. Worst of all it was covered in graffiti and dirt.

We clambered onto the train and were able to find a compartment with two empty, worn, and chewing gum encrusted seats. I managed to place the roll-a-board in an overhead rack and took my seat, facing Bertie. He, in turn, sat there holding onto the box containing Jenny's urn as if it were a newborn baby. The train ultimately pulled away from the station, and we inched ever so slowly toward Victoria Station.

Bertie was uncharacteristically quiet on the trip from Gatwick to his flat – at least other than for a half hour-long discourse on the history of Victoria Station. But even that was delivered in a subdued manner.

Even if I had wanted to listen to Bertie's monologue, it would have been difficult to impossible. It seemed as if everyone on the train had cell phones – or "mobiles" as the English insist on calling them, and each had either received or placed a call at the same time. With a train car full of people yelling into their cell phones, the noise level was incredible. Twenty-five years ago you could have heard a pin drop when riding the train or tube. On this day you would have trouble hearing yourself think. All I could think was that stuffy old England had definitely changed, for the worse – if that was possible.

The tube ride proved to be a repeat of the one experienced on the train, if not worse. Emerging from a putrid and decrepit underground station, and leaving the awful cell phone chatter behind, we walked the block or so to Bertie's flat – Bertie still carrying Jenny's urn, me dragging the roll-a-board.

A light rain was falling but that hadn't cleared the sidewalks of people. Every few yards there seemed to be clusters of humanity, huddled in groups in doorways and engaged in animated conversations. A few of them stopped talking when they saw Bertie, giving him the faintest hint of a greeting – and me an icy stare.

But these were definitely a different type of people than those who had been here in 1972. The proper Englishman in his jacket, wrinkled white shirt, and narrow dark tie seemed to have vanished, to be replaced by an astonishing number of Middle Easterners – virtually all of whom were men. Bertie and I appeared to be the only white faces on the street.

The neighborhood, which had been a bit shop-worn my last trip, now looked like some third world nation. Like the train stations we had passed on our journey from Gatwick, there was dirt, garbage and graffiti everywhere. A staggering number of crude, handwritten posters were affixed to walls, mailboxes, and lampposts. Again, however, Bertie seemed oblivious to the chaos about us.

Bertie's flat had, with one significant exception, hardly changed since my last visit. It was just as gloomy, chilly, and cramped as I remembered. I couldn't even begin to imagine what it must have been like to spend thirty long years there.

The one alteration to the living quarters was a flock of cheaply constructed bookcases and file cabinets. They were on every wall of the living room, making the already diminutive flat seem even smaller. Either Bertie or his mother had been doing a lot of heavy reading over the past few decades. My bet was on Bertie.

Bertie pointed out what would be my bedroom for the night, his mother's former room, and suggested I deposit my luggage there. I opened the bedroom door and parked the roll-a-board in a corner.

The bedroom contained a narrow bed, nightstand, wardrobe and dressing table — but no bookcases or file cabinets, only a mountain of magazines stacked carefully on the floor next to the bed. All were, evidently, magazines about English royalty. Based on the stale smell that had engulfed me when I had entered, I suspected that the door to the room hadn't been opened in months. My spirits sank with the thought of spending the night there.

Returning to the living room, I watched as Bertie, his back to me, tenderly placed Jenny's cardboard box on a small coffee table in the living room. He then took a seat on the chair next to it, removed his glasses and brushed away what I suspected was a tear from his eye. It was only then that he realized I had returned. He quickly regained his composure.

"We'll leave tomorrow morning, Vince. You'll need a good night's rest after that long plane ride. But you best stay up till regular bedtime here, as I understand that's the proper way to deal with jet lag. Besides, we've got a lot of catching up to do. Have a seat and let's chat."

My mind reeled at that thought, but I nodded my head and took a seat on the couch. "You said you would make arrangements for a car. Where and when do we pick it up?"

"It's been taken care of," said Bertie, a strange faraway look in his eyes. "It's been taken care of; so don't you worry." With that he stood up and walked, grim-faced, to the window, the only window of the flat that faced the street. He stared into the distance for perhaps two minutes, then, shaking his head, turned to me. I feared a long discourse coming. I wasn't wrong.

"See those people out there?" asked Bertie, "Did you notice that not one of them is English?"

"Well," I answered, "they may not be the direct descendants of your Druids, Celts, Normans, or Anglo-Saxons, but I would guess they are English."

Bertie's eyebrows arched and he gave me a pitying look. "Perhaps on paper; perhaps on paper. But, sure as there's a God in Heaven, they aren't English in my eyes. Just look at them. They still dress like they did in the country they came from. Most still speak their native language – and damn few of them consider themselves English. Vince, you can walk for blocks and not see more than a handful of white faces.

I tried to restrain myself. I tried even harder not to let it show that the little bigot offended me. One thing I had learned in my previous encounters with Bertie was that there was little point in arguing with the man. It only prolonged his diatribes.

"Vince," Bertie continued, "did you notice the park across the street? There's graffiti, and worse, on every bench. Do you know what some of *those* people do? They actually trap and eat the birds, particularly the pigeons. Vince, those are not civilized human beings."

Clearly Bertie hadn't been as oblivious to the environment outside his flat as I had thought.

For the next hour or so Bertie lambasted his neighbors, moaned on about the dismal future of his country, damned the influx of American fast food joints, fumed about the EU, carped about the switch to the metric system, lamented the loss of manners in his country, and claimed that "those foreigners," as he called them, would be the downfall of England. Through it all I managed to maintain my silence, a prisoner in the tiny apartment. The thought of having to share a car with Bertie the next few days became more and more alarming.

"Bertie, jet lag or not, I've really got to get some sleep." I stood up, about to retreat to the sanctuary of the bedroom.

"I understand, Vince. But, before you do that we really do need to talk about the trip. Did you bring the painting?"

"No, Bertie, I didn't bring the painting, but I did have a full-sized color print made of it. I thought that a print would be easier to cart around the country. It's in my suitcase. Let me get it."

I placed the print on the kitchen table. Jenny's mother had painted the original when Jenny was about eight. It was quite beautiful, capturing an almost fairy tale landscape scene. In its center was a small church bathed in golden sunlight. To the left of the church, perhaps a hundred feet or so, was a cobalt blue brook. Two children were pictured on the bank of the stream. One, a chubby red-haired boy, was fishing. The other, a fair and delicate looking little girl, was picking wildflowers. The boy was supposedly Bertie, the girl, Jenny.

"Ah yes, that's the one. That's the church. It's been a long time but I do remember this painting. So it's there that our dear Jenny wants to rest?" Bertie said, pointing to the graveyard to the rear of the little church.

"Yes, just moments before she passed away she pointed to the painting. Her last words to me were that I bury her there. I only wish she would have been able to tell me just where in the whole of England that little church might be located."

"Don't you worry, Vince, we'll find it. But I've got to ask you something. Jenny died nearly two years ago. Why is it that it's only now that you've brought her back for a proper burial?"

"You know, Bertie, you talk way too much. Way too damn much." A look of surprise and hurt came over Bertie's face. I strode to the bedroom and closed the door, immediately regretting my outburst.

4

SATURDAY MORNING, 19 APRIL 1997:
LONDON; THE QUEST BEGINS

The mounting din from the constant stream of cars, lorries, buses and ever so chatty people beneath the bedroom window woke me from a sound sleep. Not even the extra dose of painkillers I had taken the night before could have blocked out the clamor. No wonder Aunt Fiona had such a sour disposition. If I had to wake up every morning to this noise I'd start yelling at people too.

I looked at my watch. It was a few minutes before 6 a.m., London time, and – judging from the dim light coming through the curtained window – it appeared as though the sun had just begun to rise. Eager to get a start on the day, I turned on the lamp beside the bed. Its twenty-watt bulb lent the tiny room an unearthly hue. If Aunt Fiona used that pathetic little lamp to read all those magazines on the floor, she must have had one hell of a pair of eyes.

I put on my bathrobe, grabbed my ditty bag, and opened the door. Bertie's bedroom door was ajar and the light coming from it illuminated the living room of his flat. I glanced into his bedroom and saw that it, like the living room, was absolutely chock-a-block with file cabinets and bookcases. Crammed into one corner was a small desk. Seated on that desk was a computer – a top of the line Dell with a twenty-inch screen. Bertie, it would seem, had embraced the

Information Age – with a vengeance. The only things missing from his jam-packed bedroom was a bed – and Bertie.

"Morning, Vince," came a gravelly morning voice behind me.

I turned to see Bertie, reclining on the couch and propped on one elbow, rubbing the sleep from his eyes. "Bertie, I didn't realize you would have to sleep on the couch. You should have told me; I would have found a room for the night. I'm really sorry; I didn't know you had made your bedroom into an office."

"Think nothing of it, old chap. I've been sleeping on this sofa for about six years – ever since I ran out of space in the bedroom. It's really quite comfortable." He reached for a robe and pointed to the door of the flat's bathroom. "Go ahead and take care of things, Vince. I'll start breakfast." Looking at the clock, he added, "My goodness, we're going to get an early start on the day. That's good; lots to do. Lots to do."

Bertie's bathroom was so tiny that it reminded me of all the tired old jokes ever made about small rooms. But it was spotless and had all the necessary prerequisites. Stepping out of the shower I detected the unmistakable aroma of a full English breakfast, and my heart sank. After my unfortunate outburst last night, however, I didn't have it in me to tell Bertie that I despised fried tomatoes, loathed watery scrambled eggs, and could not stomach what passed for bacon in this sad country.

Bertie had set the table and poured tiny glasses of orange juice for the both of us. A big smile on his face, he remarked, "Have a seat, Vince; everything's ready." So I did, hoping that a full English breakfast may not have been quite as bad as I remembered. Unfortunately, it was worse.

In addition to the tomatoes, eggs, and bacon, Bertie had prepared tea, mushrooms, beans, fried bread, and black slabs of something I didn't recognize. Other than the hot tea and black slabs, which were only barely edible, everything else –

including the "orange juice" – was just ghastly. Trying to be polite, I decided to ask him about the black slabs.

"Excellent breakfast, Bertie." His face lit up. "This meat or sausage, or whatever, was particularly tasty," I remarked, pointing at the last scrap of the black slabs.

"Ah," said Bertie, "so you like my black pudding. That's wonderful; most Yanks tend to shy away from it."

"Why's that?" I asked, hoping I could stomach the answer.

"I don't really know, Vince. I suppose it's just that the idea of eating congealed pig's blood wrapped in a length of pig's intestine puts some people off. You'd really think that a country that believes hotdogs are edible wouldn't be so squeamish." Pleased to no end by that witty observation, Bertie gave me a wink and shoveled in another spoonful of watery eggs.

I started to say something, thought better of it, and just nodded my head. Not much point in yelling at the man. Based on the amount of blood pudding he had ingested it was clear that Cousin Bertie considered the black garbage a delicacy.

When we were first married, Jenny had tried to tempt me with a full English breakfast. That had resulted in our first spat. She was never able to convince me that English food was anything but sad garbage, although I have to admit that she did manage to train me to use certain English expressions. To this day the hood of a car is a "bonnet;" the trunk is a "boot;" and we always stopped at "petrol" stations, rather than gas stations, to have the car fueled or serviced. I never could, however, bring myself to call a wrench a "spanner" or a cookie a "biscuit."

It took Bertie at least two hours to wash, shave, dress and finish packing. I had the uneasy feeling that he wasn't really in a hurry to get this particular show on the road. It was ultimately agreed that we were going to be taking the print of the church, Jenny's urn, two suitcases, and three cardboard book boxes on our expedition.

"Bertie, what's with the boxes? Are we going to have room enough for all this?"

"I've got notes and reference materials in the boxes, Vince, and lots of ordnance survey maps. We'll need them if we're going to find that church. Mark my words."

I shrugged my shoulders, deciding not to argue with him. "So, where do we pick up the car?"

"Abdul should be around any minute now," said Bertie, looking at the clock over the kitchen stove. It was almost 10 a.m. I didn't ask who Abdul was.

At precisely 10 a.m. there was a single, sharp knock on the rear door of the flat. Bertie opened the door and I could see two men, one evidently an Arab, the other a tall, muscular black man. Both seemed delighted to see Bertie. Both eyed me with suspicion.

The Arab was indeed Abdul. The black man was named Nigel. Judging from his accent, I guessed he was from some Caribbean island, probably Jamaica.

Between the four of us we gathered up the suitcases and boxes. Nigel, effortlessly carrying two of the book boxes, headed out the back door, down the rickety steps, and into the rear garden. The rest of us followed his lead.

There was a small alley directly behind the garden, a place where I would have expected the rental car to be parked. There wasn't, however, an automobile in sight. Instead of heading toward the alley, Nigel strode purposely toward an ancient, dilapidated garden shed and placed his boxes on the ground. Abdul put his box down and tossed Nigel a huge brass key, roughly the size of a man's fist. Nigel then quickly opened the oversize lock on the door of the shed, grinning like a madman, his teeth flashing in the morning light.

There wasn't a single garden tool in the shed, but there was what appeared to be an undersized car – covered for the moment in old bed sheets. Nigel walked to one side of the car, Abdul to the other. They looked to Bertie, who simply nodded his head. On the count of three the two men removed the covering with a flourish. All that was missing was a drum roll.

What I saw when the sheets were removed literally took my breath away. It was a small, incredibly shiny black car – appearing to be a relic from either the thirties or, at best, post Second World War. I was speechless.

Abdul broke the silence. "So, Professor, how do you like it? Quite a beauty, don't you think?"

"It is definitely beautiful," I responded, and I meant it. "But do you think a car of this age is going to be reliable … and safe?" The smiles disappeared from the faces of Abdul and Nigel. I had clearly committed a major *faux pas*.

I turned to Bertie, who just rolled his eyes. "Vince, this is quite possibly the finest motorcar ever manufactured. This, my dear man, is a 1949 two-door Morris Minor MM Saloon. Abdul and Nigel have spent months of nights and weekends working on the car. It's been licensed, registered, and road tested. It may be a little long in the tooth, but it will take us anywhere we want to go, and quite reliably and safely I'm sure."

Nigel chimed in. "Only eight thousand miles on the car, mon, and those are brand new tires. Michelins. Brand new hoses and fan belts too." Abdul nodded in agreement.

Bertie, his face now red with either anger or embarrassment, walked to the front of the car and opened the bonnet. Inside was the smallest engine I had ever seen in an automobile.

"This," Bertie said, pointing to the pint-sized engine, "is a 918cc sidevalve engine – arguably the most reliable engine ever produced. This car has an Alta DIY conversion kit giving it a top speed of 78 mph and a 0-60 time of 20.4 seconds. All that and 40 mpg on the highway." With that he slammed the bonnet shut.

A top speed of 78 mph? A 0-60 time of 20.4 seconds? My God, I thought, we'd have trouble racing a snail. Yet Bertie and his two lunatic chums seemed to think this relic of the forties was safe to drive on the motorways of the nineties.

Abdul and Nigel's eyes shifted from Bertie to me as they waited expectantly for my response. The downcast looks on the faces of the two men made protest futile. I surrendered. "Gentlemen, I didn't mean to insult anyone. I sincerely apologize. The car will be fine. In fact, I'm looking forward to the drive."

The smiles returned to the faces of Abdul and Nigel. Bertie simply looked tired.

We packed the suitcases and Jenny's carton into the boot of the car. The three book boxes had to be placed on the rear seat. I was about to shake Nigel's hand when he pulled out a brass whistle, placed the business end in his mouth, and gave it a powerful blow. I didn't know quite what to make of it. Either the big fellow didn't care for handshakes or he was signaling for the cops.

From seemingly out of nowhere a crowd gathered. There were Blacks, Asians, Middle Easterners, and a matched pair of elderly white women. The group ranged in age from infants to octogenarians. They were all smiling.

I was introduced to the assembly, most of whom were relatives of either Nigel or Abdul. The two old women were twin sisters and, according to Bertie, had resided in a nearby apartment building for over seventy years. They had been drinking buddies of Bertie until the neighborhood pub had been turned into a tobacco shop some five or so years ago.

The pretty young woman in a headscarf who had been introduced as Abdul's wife handed me a wicker picnic basket. Nigel's wife gave Bertie a large, crudely labeled bottle of what I later found out was homemade rum. I placed the picnic basket securely on top of the book boxes. Bertie held tightly to the bottle of rum. He clearly had no intention of letting it out of his sight.

Satisfied that we were well provisioned, each member of the crowd gave both Bertie and me a hug and kiss. Bertie's lower lip quivered for a brief moment. Nigel and Abdul, on the other hand, totally lost it. It was as if they were never going to see us again. Either that or the sobbing pair had less confidence in the ancient Morris Minor than they had let on. The only other reason I could come up with was almost unthinkable; the two men actually cared that deeply for Bertie.

Nigel, sniffling, gave me one last bear hug and handed me the car keys. I checked to see if any ribs had been broken and then got into the shiny old relic. I snapped on the seat belt – a feature that had been added, as an afterthought, by Abdul – and placed the key in the ignition and gave it a twist. The motor turned over smoothly, all four Lilliputian cylinders of the 918cc sidevalve engine giving it their very best. It gave one the impression of a smooth running sewing machine housed under the bonnet. Bertie, however, just stood outside the car, staring dumbly at the passenger-side door handle. I reached over and opened the door, impatient to be on our way.

"Get in, Bertie. We really need to be leaving." Bertie stood firm for a moment and then, quite reluctantly, got into the car. The man's face was pale; his brow was sweating. Even his hands were trembling. He gave a weak wave to the crowd of well-wishers and off we drove.

The drive out of London was harrowing. This was my first ever experience in attempting to drive on the left side of the road – and it showed. Bertie, to his credit, only gave out sporadic yelps of fright. Considering that the little car was forty-eight years old and had no air bags, I shared his concern.

"Bertie, would you prefer to drive?"

"Oh no, I haven't driven a motorcar in years. Besides, I don't have a license. You're doing just fine; I'm just here to map out the course," said Bertie, his hands still trembling.

Leaving London we entered the A2 road, heading in the direction of Canterbury. By then it was past one in the afternoon. "Bertie, what's our destination?"

Bertie, seeming to have recovered his composure somewhat, replied. "We're first going to visit the pleasant little village of Lower Friththingden. We need to travel about sixty miles more on this motorway, and then roughly eight more miles on a side road. Our families used to sometimes stay over in this particular village when Jenny and I were children. So we'll just see if Jenny's church is there."

"How did you plan this out?" I asked. "I mean, how did you go about determining our route?"

Bertie's brow furrowed. He seemed to be giving a fairly simple question an inordinate amount of thought. Finally, he responded.

"Our two families, mine and Jenny's, always took their vacations together – at least until Jenny and her mother moved to the States. We'd travel the countryside, from one small village to the next. Lower Friththingden was sometimes one of our stops. If we stopped over at any place long enough, Jenny's mother would get out her easel and paints. So I just marked off some likely villages along the routes we usually took. I'm sure that Jenny's church has to be in one of them."

"Sounds reasonable. I'm counting on you, Bertie."

Bertie seemed to squirm in his seat. I suppose I was putting too much pressure on the man.

Once we were about thirty or so miles outside London there was a noticeable change in the scenery. We left the horrendous traffic and the dirt and grime of the city and its suburbs and entered a relatively pleasant – at least for England – countryside. The day was sunny and mild. The sky was, with the exception of a few fluffy clouds, clear blue. It was a nice surprise. In my previous two visits to England it had never stopped raining, and I had never ventured more than a few miles outside the city.

"Vince, why don't you pull over," Bertie said, pointing to an open spot on the side of the road. "It's past lunch time and we'd best enjoy our picnic lunch before it goes off."

As impatient as I was to get on with things I decided to humor Bertie. I parked the Morris Minor in the spot he had pointed out and turned off the engine. Bertie was out of the car before it had come to a complete stop. Rather obviously, Bertie was not one for car trips.

Standing alongside the car, Bertie took it on himself to educate me further on the wonders of a 1949 Morris Minor.

"Vince, see that piece of metal in the middle of the front bumper? It actually joins the two pieces that make up the bumper. Any idea why the bumper isn't in one piece?"

I had to admit that I hadn't the foggiest, but I knew that I soon would.

"Alex Issigonis designed this truly amazing motorcar when he worked at the Morris Company. When he drove the first prototype, back in 1948, he realized that the design was a bit too narrow. So, mainly for aesthetic purposes mind you, he decided to make the car four inches wider. There was one problem though; the Morris firm had already manufactured thousands of bumpers. This didn't stop Issigonis. He simply had the bumpers cut in half and added this bumper-widening device. Brilliant, don't you think? Any Morris Minor with that piece was made before 1951." By the time he had finished his monologue Bertie was beaming, an expectant look on his face, awaiting my reaction.

I digested the facts and responded. "Fascinating. But tell me, Bertie, where did Abdul and Nigel locate this antique?"

"They didn't 'locate' it. It's been sitting in the garden shed behind my flat for thirty years."

"Then this was your parent's car ... the one that was in the accident?" I asked.

Bertie's face flushed. I had hit a nerve.

For a moment Bertie was silent, then he responded, his words slow and deliberate. "That's right, the very same one. As Jenny probably told you, we were forced off the road by a lorry. Mum was sitting in the passenger side seat and was thrown from the car. Father was in the back seat. The motorcar itself had a few dents and scratches, but that was it. My parents, however, didn't fare as well. Father's neck was broken and Mum suffered a shattered hip. Ever since then the vehicle has been in the shed, at least until Abdul and Nigel agreed to put it in running order."

"Abdul and Nigel seemed like nice guys. They sure seem to think highly of you."

"They are wonderful chaps; top notch," said Bertie.

"Isn't that something of a contradiction, Bertie? Back in your flat you went on and on about how all these foreigners and foreign ideas are going to destroy England. Yet your two best friends are foreigners."

Bertie seemed perplexed by the question and chose to change the subject. "Vince, we really need to eat our lunch and get back on the road."

5

SATURDAY AFTERNOON, 19 APRIL 1997:
THE ERRANT HUN

The picnic lunch was wonderful, not so much as a hint of English food until Bertie insisted on putting a dab of some awful concoction called Marmite on his falafel. He had evidently packed several jars of the foul smelling stuff in one of his "book" boxes. Some reference material, I thought.

Finished with the picnic lunch, we made our way to Lower Friththingden, reaching the outskirts of the village in the late afternoon. Lower Friththingden couldn't have had more than a few hundred inhabitants, and nothing about the place would seem to place it in a "must see" status. It was quaint in a plain, old-fashioned sort of way, but so were most of the other villages we had passed on the main highway. I could only wonder what might have drawn Bertie and Jenny's parents to this rather ordinary place.

The spire of the village church, evidently the only church in Lower Friththingden, was clearly visible, and seemed to be located in the very center of the village. Its tall, ornate spire, however, looked nothing at all like that of the unpretentious little church in the painting.

"Bertie, if that's the only church around here, then we're definitely not in the right place."

"Oh, there must be other churches," said Bertie. "Here's my suggestion. Drop me off at the local pub; then you drive about and see if you come across any other churches. In the meantime, I'll show the print to the locals in the pub and see if they recognize it."

I wasn't sure that it made much sense to drive aimlessly about the countryside but decided not to argue. Besides, I was sure that Bertie was looking for more than information in the pub, and I never cared for either English beer or smoke filled pubs.

There appeared to be only two pubs in the village and Bertie insisted on being deposited in front of the one on the village outskirts, a nondescript red brick building housing a pub called the *Errant Hun*. He took the print and a small manila envelope with him.

I drove through the village and toured the back roads in the vicinity. I would have to admit that the countryside was picturesque, but the only buildings to be seen were farmhouses and farm buildings. Convinced that there was no other church in the area, I drove back to the village and parked the Morris Minor near the *Errant Hun*.

The car immediately drew a crowd, or at least what probably passed for a crowd in that vicinity. One fellow, most likely the village idiot, even pointed out the bumper-widening device that Bertie had raved on about. I excused myself and made for the village square. For the next hour or so I walked the streets and took in the sights, such as they were.

The one thing that stood out about the place was the difference, other than for the obvious disparity in size, between the village and London. To me, London had always seemed dreary and grimy. The attractions seemed contrived, maintained for the benefit of the tourist industry. But this village was *real*. It was not some prop for tourists; instead it was a village designed solely to support the lives and livelihoods of its inhabitants. That in itself was refreshing. Other than that it seemed a dull place, full – I guessed – of dull people.

Checking my wristwatch I noticed that it was going on 7 p.m. and decided to rendezvous with Cousin Bertie. It had just occurred to me that we had no place to stay for the night, and an all too familiar pain was beginning to seep through my joints.

I entered the *Errant Hun* and it was, as I had feared, smoke-filled and smelling of stale beer. I didn't see Bertie anywhere and decided to check with the bartender, a pencil-thin, middle-aged man with an enormous nose and seemingly no chin.

"Was there a fellow in here earlier; a short, red-haired stocky man wearing a tweed cap?" I asked.

"Oh, you must mean Bertie," replied the emaciated bartender. The others at the bar all nodded, with the most sober of the bunch saying something to the effect that Bertie was one hilariously funny bloke. Oddly enough, he seemed to mean it as a compliment. The bartender leaned over the bar and pointed in the direction of the far corner of the pub. "That would be him there, talking with our Tom Hawkes. They've been at it for some time now."

I turned and spotted Bertie in the corner, his back to me. But how, I wondered, did everyone at the bar seem to know him? He couldn't have been in the pub more than a few hours.

"So, are you fellows and Bertie old friends?" I asked.

"Oh no," came the reply from a pale old gent nursing a pint of equally pale ale. "We just met him this day. One fine chap, that Bertie." Everyone nodded in agreement. This was yet another reaction to Bertie-the-bore I had never seen or expected.

I swung around on the bar stool so as to get a better look at the *Errant Hun's* most popular customer. Seated across from Bertie was a white haired gentleman with a pair of clear plastic tubes stuck up his nose. The other end of the tubes led to an oxygen tank seated on a cart directly behind the man. The fellow the bartender called Tom was evidently suffering from emphysema, or worse. Yet there he was sitting in a cloud of smoke and chatting away with Bertie.

Bertie and Tom seemed engaged in some heavy conversation and I decided not to interrupt. Instead I decided to take a chance on an English beer. The bartender recommended the local bitter and poured me a half pint. It wasn't half bad.

"I've been wondering," I said, my remarks directed to the bartender, "about the name of this place. Why the *Errant Hun?*"

The others at the bar rolled their eyes. The bartender sighed, reached under the counter and handed me a well-worn laminated sheet. The heading on the top was "A Brief History of the *Errant Hun.*"

Reading the sheet, I discovered that the *Errant Hun* had been built in 1946, over the foundation of an earlier pub that had been called the *Sow and Centipede.* According to the write up, the *Sow and Centipede* had been obliterated during the Second World War by a German parachute mine. It was conjectured that the crew of an errant German bomber, flying blind through thick cloud cover and unable to locate their primary target, had randomly and maliciously dropped the parachute mine before returning to their home base.

"Good grief," I remarked, "any casualties?"

The bartender reached for the sheet, placed it back under the bar, and replied. "No, not a soul lost. Almost everyone in the village was at church that afternoon, attending the Christmas play put on by the village children. That play likely saved the life of a number of thirsty villagers. Damn lucky, that lot. And damn lucky for me as my own father would have been in the *Sow and Centipede* had it not been for the play."

"And," said the old gent nursing the pint of pale ale, "this village would have been spared the likes of you." This remark struck the crowd as sidesplitting. One of the village drunks even spewed beer through his nostrils. The bartender just glared at the old gent.

I moved to a seat at the end of the bar, where I could get a better view of Bertie and Tom. They were now huddled over, their faces no more than a few inches apart. Tom seemed excited, and he appeared to be doing most of the talking. Bertie just kept nodding his head. Yet another side of Bertie I had not seen before.

After about ten minutes Bertie handed Tom a manila envelope. Tom, in turn, opened the envelope, pulled out a thick wad of pound notes, and replaced them with what looked like photographs. He then handed the envelope back to Bertie. The man then reached inside his jacket and retrieved what looked like a tobacco tin. He handed the tin to Bertie, who placed it in his own jacket pocket. This was just too weird. Cousin Bertie would have some questions to answer this evening. Then again, the danger in asking Bertie a question was that he would give you an answer, one that would go on for hours.

Bertie reached across the table and shook hands with Tom. He rose from his seat, turned around, and started walking toward the bar. The moment he saw me the look on his face changed abruptly, like a kid with his hand caught in the cookie jar.

"Lo, Vince. Didn't expect you back so soon." Then, recovering his composure, he added "I was able to find a B&B for the night, about five miles down the main road. Freddie, the bartender, already called ahead. They even agreed to prepare dinner for us. We'd best be on our way."

I nodded, deciding to save my questions for later. We left the *Errant Hun* and walked to the Morris Minor. Once again Bertie seemed reluctant to get in. Finally, he sucked in his breath and gingerly opened the passenger door. He placed the church print back into one of the boxes in the rear of the car. I turned the key and, just as before, the tiny engine came to life. Abdul and Nigel had done their work well.

#####

"So, Bertie, did anyone in the pub recognize the church?"

"The church? Oh, you mean the print. No, no one claimed to have ever seen it."

"Hmm. Based on the amount of time you were spending with the white-haired fellow in the corner, I thought for sure you had some leads."

"No, sorry about that. I just discovered that Tom, the chap you were referring to, shared my interest in military history. He's a Second World War buff, knows all sorts of interesting things. Did you know, Vince, that one particular B17 – a Flying Fortress named *Old Gappy* – flew 157 missions! Can you imagine that? What do you think the probability was of a B17 completing even fifty missions? I'll tell you …"

I had to interrupt. "Bertie, I'm not really interested in B17s or the Second World War. We're here to find the church in the painting; nothing more, nothing less." Bertie went quiet.

We arrived at the B&B while it was still light. It was a small, tidy house with a well-manicured front garden. I parked on the street and we unloaded everything except the book boxes and empty picnic basket. Bertie resisted at first, but I convinced him that there was no way that I was going to lug book boxes in and out of our lodgings each stop.

The B&B was run by a husband and wife, both in their early to mid thirties. He had been an investment banker in London, she a stewardess for British Air. Both had decided to give up life in the city for the peace and solitude of the countryside. They claimed to be thrilled with their new life. But then, I would suppose that just escaping London itself would be enough to make anyone giddy.

The dinner they prepared for us was simple but passable. Meat, potatoes, and carrots accompanied by a rather decent red wine. Bertie inhaled a first helping, raced through a second, and finished with a third. The man could certainly put away the food.

When the meal was finished Bertie and I helped clear the table. The couple refused our offer to help with the dishes, insisting that we all retire to their parlor. Brandy was served, prompting Bertie to give a mini-lecture on the history of the liquor.

Surprisingly, either the couple found Bertie's discourse interesting or else they were incredibly polite. Even more surprisingly, Bertie didn't talk the subject to death. Soon he and the couple were engaged in conversation, ranging from investment banking to flying to running a B&B. Feeling a bit the odd man out, I excused myself and went to my bedroom. Fortunately, the B&B had separate rooms for Bertie and me, and thus I was assured at least one Bertie-free night.

From my roll-a-board I retrieved the box containing my assortment of pills. The level of pain this day had been worse than usual, and I decided to take the acetaminophen-codeine in addition to the other medications. Despite the warnings on the bottle about driving while using this combination, there was no way I would be able to get through the night without it.

6
SUNDAY, 20 APRIL 1997:
THE WHITE CLIFFS OF DOVER

Despite the painkillers, I endured a restless and uncomfortable night. The bed was lumpy and at least a half foot too short for my six foot two inch body. As a result I spent most of the night thinking about Jenny, wishing that I had spent more time with her – even wishing that I had accompanied her on her yearly visits to England. My excuse had been my research. My real reason had been that I simply could not stomach either England or the English. Given the choice between living in England or Hell, I would have had to give the matter serious thought.

I only wish that I had been man enough to put up with England for the sake of being with Jenny. After all, she had once told me that, while I would always be her first love, her second was the land where she had been born and raised. Why, oh why, had I been such a stubborn, selfish fool?

At first light I got up, discovering that every joint in my body was stiff and sore. The bed had done its worst. I found my robe and ditty bag, opened the bedroom door, and walked down the hall to the shared bath. It, unfortunately, was already occupied. I decided to wait for the occupant, who I assumed was Bertie, to finish. Within a few minutes a well-scrubbed Bertie emerged from the bathroom, giving me a big smile.

"Wonderful place this, eh what? Slept like a baby last night. How about you, Vince?"

"Yeah," I lied, "me too. Like a baby."

My little fib seemed to please Bertie. Beaming with satisfaction, he started down the hall to his bedroom.

"Bertie, where next? What's our next stop?"

Bertie paused, turned around, and replied. "We'll be off to Haywards Heath next; it's a small town south of London – not that far from Gatwick where your plane landed. But, Vince, would it be okay if we made a slight detour? We're not that far from Dover, and I'd really love to see the white cliffs."

I wasn't in any mood to take a detour, even a "slight" one. However, the sad, puppy dog look on Bertie's face made refusal impossible. "Okay, we'll take your detour. But let's not waste time there; we've got a church to find."

"No worry. All I want to do is take a quick look. After all, the white cliffs of Dover are something that every good Englishman should see at least once in his lifetime. I promise not to tarry," said Bertie.

"All right, then it's settled. We take a quick side trip to those white cliffs of yours; then it's back to business," I replied.

"Wonderful. I'll meet you downstairs for breakfast. Toodle loo."

The bathroom was, in a word, quaint. There was a small sink and an ancient, and evidently genuine "Thomas Crapper" complete with pull chain. But no tub or shower. The sink had those damnably insane English faucets – one tap for hot water, another for cold. You had the choice of either scalding yourself, or washing with freezing water, or filling the filthy basin with a mixture of the two. I had no intention of the latter, so I washed with cold water. If nothing else, it sharpened the senses.

I dressed, packed and headed downstairs – hoping to skip another awful full English breakfast. Bertie and my hosts, however, were so adamant that I eat something before departing that I finally agreed to have some toast and tea.

The couple walked us to the car after breakfast. They shook my hand and wished me the best. Bertie, however, was given a warm embrace by the man – something that I had never seen an Englishman do – followed by a hug and kiss from the woman. Bertie gave them his address and phone number in London and they assured him that they would drop by the next time they were in the city. They seemed sincere. They were obviously insane.

Following Bertie's instructions, I followed the signs leading to Dover. According to his calculations, the drive should take less than an hour. I could only hope he was right as I was anxious to get back to the business at hand, and a trip to the white cliffs wasn't part of that business.

Once we arrived, I found a parking spot near a pathway that followed the rim of the white cliffs. Bertie exited the car and literally raced toward the path, coming to a sudden stop at a sign warning of the danger of proceeding farther.

"Ah, Vince," said Bertie as I approached him, "isn't this a lovely view? Someday we'll have to return here and do our visit justice. What I'd really like is to take a ferry to the continent, and then back. Wouldn't it be wonderful to have a glimpse of these cliffs from the sea? Ah, it must be a grand sight."

Before giving me a chance to answer, he cleared his throat and began a recitation:

I have loved England, dearly and deeply;
Since that first morning, shining and pure;
The white cliffs of Dover I saw rising steeply;
Out of the sea that once made her secure.

"This visit has brought out the poet in you, Bertie."

"Oh no, that's not *my* poem. Those are the first lines of 'The White Cliffs,' by Alice Duer Miller. Surely you've read it."

"I'm afraid not," I replied.

"Well then, you *must* have heard the song," said Bertie, a perplexed look on his face.

"What song is that?" I asked, wondering just where this would lead.

To my astonishment, Bertie started singing. As I recall, the first verse went something like:

There'll be blue birds over
The white cliffs of Dover
Tomorrow, just you wait and see.

The song included references to shepherds tending sheep and Jimmy going to sleep in his own little room again, but I've got to admit to being too perplexed by Bertie's singing to give it my full attention.

"There, now, you must have heard that song at least once in your life," said Bertie. "I do believe that it was one of Jenny's favorites."

"You're right, I've never knew the words before but I have definitely heard the tune. Jenny used to hum it. Of course her rendition was a bit more on key than yours."

Bertie ignored the dig. "Alice Duer Miller's poem inspired the song. Both the poem and song came out in the early forties, right at the beginning of the war. The song is quite wonderful, don't you think?"

By this time I was thoroughly sick of the white cliffs, tired of wasting time and eager to get back to business – and that likely had some influence on my reply. "I never realized that you English could be so sentimental. Nor write such utter drivel."

"Oh, we can be sentimental. But the credit for both the poem and song has to go to a pair of Yanks. Alice Duer Miller was born on Staten Island, New York. The chap who composed the song was Nat Burton, an American who had never even visited our fair land. And I would hardly say that either works are utter drivel," said Bertie, a hurt look on his face.

"I apologize," I replied, wishing that I could learn to keep my big mouth shut.

We walked back to the car in silence. I was afraid that my apology had been woefully insufficient, but I couldn't think of anything more to add. So I decided to take the cowardly way out and change the subject.

"Bertie, I think we should make a few stops along the route. We can check in pubs along the way and see if anyone knows where Jenny's church is located, just as you did back in Lower Friththingden."

I was surprised by his reaction. He finally agreed, but didn't seem particularly enthused with the idea. He did warn me that, this being a Sunday, pubs would not open until noon.

As I headed the car back to the motorway Bertie reached behind him and retrieved a book from one of the boxes in the backseat. Glancing over I could see that it was a manual on bird watching, complete with color photographs. For the next two hours he spent his time commenting on the birds he spotted on either side of the motorway. He ultimately went almost berserk upon sighting what he described as a rare hen harrier. And he really came close to losing it when I remarked that the bird looked like nothing more than a hawk. Shaking his head in disgust, he spent the next half hour describing the feeding and mating habits of what I found to be a rather disgusting fowl.

The first pub we stopped at was the *Perplexed Parson* in the town of Bexhill. We entered the establishment and Bertie made a beeline for the bar. I decided to try my luck with an elderly gentleman who was at the moment wolfing down a Ploughman's lunch of bread, cheese, and pickles – accompanied by a pint of beer. I walked to his table and stood there for a moment, trying to come up with an opening line. After thirty seconds or so he finally paused and looked up, gracing me with a stony stare.

"Hello," I said, putting on a happy face. "My friend and I are looking for a church." I unrolled the print and placed it on the table. "It's the one in this picture. Might you have seen this particular church?"

The old gent took a quick glance at the print, shook his head, and went back to his meal. I tried the same line with a couple at the next table, with pretty much the same, snotty response. One woman, in fact, informed me that a pub was an odd place to be inquiring about a church. Damn, but the English are an insufferable people.

Defeated, I took an empty seat in the rear of the pub and decided to watch Bertie. He had ordered his second pint and was engaged in conversation with the bartender. They were both grinning. Within a few minutes a small crowd gathered, with Bertie at its epicenter. Everybody seemed to be having a swell time. I just hoped that Bertie would remember to mention the church.

After about a half hour of laughing and backslapping, Bertie excused himself. He walked to where I was seated and asked for the print. He took it back to the group and each one took a long, careful look at the scene. In fact, the old gent I had first encountered even walked to the bar and asked to see the print. That truly ticked me off. All I could figure out was that the English simply don't want to waste their precious time on anyone with an American accent. The feeling, old chums, is mutual.

A few minutes later Bertie returned to my table and suggested we move on to the next pub. I asked him if anyone had any ideas on where Jenny's church was located.

"No," he responded. "One chap thought it looked a lot like a church in the south of Yorkshire, but then he admitted that the Yorkshire church had no brook running alongside. But we'll find it, Vince, don't you worry. We'll find it."

Bertie and I walked out to the parking lot, followed by virtually everyone who had been in the pub. "I told them about the Morris Minor," whispered Bertie, without elaboration. I felt a little like the Pied Piper, ridding the pub of drunks instead of rats.

Bertie pointed out the various features of our car while the crowd listened in rapt attention. Finally, reluctantly, he shook hands all around. He got in the car, sighed, and we proceeded to motor down the highway, looking for the next village, and the next pub.

We stopped at two more pubs before closing hours curtailed that opportunity. The response was the same. I got absolutely nowhere with the locals. They acted, in fact, as if I were contagious or, even worse, French. Bertie, of course, had them eating out of his hand, but no one knew anything about the church. At each departure Bertie showed off the Morris Minor, shook hands, exchanged phone numbers, and then off we drove.

It was about 6 p.m. when we arrived at the town of Haywards Heath. It was considerably larger than Lower Friththingden and utterly devoid of charm. Bertie pointed out a promising looking B&B with a vacancy sign, and I parked the car on the street. We registered for the last two available rooms and unpacked the luggage.

"Vince, why don't we do as before? You drive around the town and its outskirts and see if you spot the church. I'll walk about and inspect the local pubs."

"Fine, but this time let's forget about B17s, the damn war, the Morris Minor, or anything else other than Jenny's church. Okay?"

Bertie looked hurt, but agreed. "Certainly. But first of all let's talk to our hosts. We can show them the print. They do look like a church-going pair."

Our hosts, an elderly couple with horrifyingly bad teeth, stared at the print for several minutes. The woman was quite sure she had never seen that particular church before. The man scratched his head, stroked his chin, and finally said that he may have seen a church like it – in a small town in Scotland. Bertie assured me that neither Jenny nor her mother had ever been to Scotland. Once again we had struck out.

At about seven in the evening, Bertie, carrying the rolled up print, left our lodgings. I started the Morris Minor, located a petrol station and filled up, and then drove the roads coming into and out of the unpleasant town of Haywards Heath. The Morris Minor continued to attract attention, and I – or, more properly, the car – received lots of waves and smiles from the locals. But the search for Jenny's church was, once again, futile.

Giving up, I drove back to the B&B and parked the car. According to our hosts, Bertie hadn't yet returned. By then it was nearly 8 p.m., and I decided to walk into the town proper and find a place to eat.

The only places, within easy walking distance, offering food were pubs and a rather oily looking fish and chips joint. I decided to save my lungs and risk my stomach on the fish. I ordered my meal and found an empty table by the front window. Within minutes the proprietor yelled out my order number, and I retrieved the plate from the counter. It looked and smelled delicious. It probably had enough cholesterol to clog the arteries of a whale, but I had to admit it was tasty. Besides, an overdose of cholesterol was the least of my worries.

I ate slowly, enjoying the meal and watching the parade of people passing by. God, they were a pale, stern looking bunch.

Just as I was finishing off the last chip, I noticed the door to a cottage directly across the street open ever so slightly. A head emerged – one topped with a familiar flat cap and red hair. It was, indeed, Cousin Bertie. He looked furtively to the left and right and, when evidently satisfied that the coast was clear, opened the door all the way. He turned and said something to someone inside, closed the door, and then walked away at a brisk pace, evidently heading back to our B&B. It was like something out of a grade B spy movie.

I sat there for a while, trying to make sense of what I had just seen. The cottage across the street was a private residence, certainly not one of the pubs that Bertie had promised to investigate. I wondered whether I should confront him, thought better of it and decided to let the matter rest for the moment. My suspicion was that Cousin Bertie had found himself a lady of the evening, possibly someone he met at a local pub. Nothing else seemed to explain the guilty look on his face when he emerged from the cottage. Bertie and his behavior were, as they say in Old Blighty, getting up my nose.

For the next half hour or so I walked the streets of the town, trying to get my head straight. Things weren't working out as I had hoped. Bertie was a puzzle. There was no doubt he loved Jenny, but he certainly didn't seem as intent on finding her church as I would have thought. Then again, he knew this country and its people far better than me – and I needed his help. Without him, I had no hope whatsoever of finding the church.

When I returned to the B&B, Bertie was holding court in the communal television room. Our elderly hosts and several of the lodgers were listening in rapt attention to one of his tired old Second World War stories – something about American deserters and a legendary "American" village – located, according to Bertie, somewhere in Britain. I walked past the crowd and straight to my bedroom, yet another tiny room with a matching undersized bed. I swallowed my painkillers and prepared myself mentally for yet another miserable night.

7
MONDAY, 21 APRIL 1997:
STANLEY AND HAZEL; BERTIE'S CONFESSION

I was awakened from a sound sleep by a sharp rap on the bedroom door. Looking at my wristwatch I was surprised to see that it was already half past seven in the morning. I was even more surprised by how good I felt. Over the past two years I could only remember a handful of relatively pain-free days. Hopefully, this was to be one of those.

"Just a minute," I shouted as I put on my robe and opened the door. Bertie was standing there, dressed and obviously anxious to get to the serious business of breakfast.

"Sorry, Bertie, I overslept. I'll get washed and shaved and join you in twenty minutes."

"No worries, old chap. I'll wait for you. I'll meet you downstairs in the dining room." Bertie then gave me a closer inspection and added, "Say, Vince, you're certainly looking well this morning. You've got some color in your face. Must have gotten over that jet lag. Got to admit it, old chap, you looked awfully tired when I met you at Gatwick."

I had no desire to get involved in a discussion on how bad or good I looked and my reply was short and to the point. "All right then, I'll see you downstairs. By the way, I assume you had no luck on your pub crawl yesterday?"

"No, sorry, I didn't find a soul who knew anything about our little church. But I'm confident that today will be a better day. Patience, old chap; one must have patience."

I could only wish that I shared his confidence. The fact that I had to actually ask him about yesterday was particularly worrisome. The search for Jenny's church just didn't seem to be making the impression on Bertie that I thought it would.

The bathroom at our current B&B had, thankfully, a shower. Not having to use the frustrating two-faucet system to wash at the sink was a welcome relief. I showered, shaved, dressed and packed before going downstairs. Finishing up, I continued to be surprised at how good I felt, and could only hope that this respite would last the day.

Bertie was seated at one of the breakfast tables, engaged in conversation with two fellow lodgers at the next table, an elderly and distinguished looking English couple. It seemed, in fact, that at every restaurant, pub, and B&B we had visited the majority of the people were approaching or perhaps even a little past their "sell by" date. It had made me wonder if there were any young people left in the countryside.

Bertie hadn't yet ordered breakfast but did have a nearly empty cup of tea in front of him. He introduced me to his new best friends, informing me that the man, Stanley, had just celebrated his 80th birthday and that he and his wife, Hazel, were on their way to a reunion in Exeter.

The birthday boy smiled, informing me that he had retired some years ago, after serving for fifty years as the doorman for a posh London hotel. In those fifty years he had only missed eight days of work. I didn't know whether I should be sad or happy for him and simply nodded. The thought of fifty years of opening and closing a door for the British upper class made the mind reel.

My lack of enthusiasm and interest seemed to embarrass Bertie. He gave me a withering look that I suppose I deserved. "Vince, Stanley has seen it all. Royalty, Prime Ministers – including Winston Churchill, actors, actresses, generals, admirals, even the Beatles. Stanley, do tell my friend the story about John Lennon."

Stanley was only too willing to oblige. Bertie, in the meantime, ordered full English breakfasts for both of us before I could stop him. I had to admit that mine wasn't all that bad, although I did refuse the group's entreaties to dab some Marmite on my toast.

Stanley regaled us with his Lennon story, followed by two Churchill vignettes, and concluded with a truly mind-boggling tale concerning Prince Philip. I have to admit that they were damn interesting. Bertie was clearly enthralled. Hazel was beaming, obviously pleased with her husband's story-telling abilities. I sat there wondering why it was that Prince Philip hadn't, years ago, been confined to an asylum – or at least kept safely locked up in the Tower of London.

Stanley paused to take a sip of tea. Finishing, he looked me directly in the eyes and asked me what I thought of England. This surprised me, as most Englishmen I had encountered shied away from asking anything close to a personal question. It also posed a quandary. If I told Stanley how I really felt about England, it would be rude and hurtful. I saw no other recourse but to lie. There was no way I wanted to offend this sweet old couple.

"It's a beautiful country," I replied. "I have to admit though, that I prefer the countryside over the big city," which was true. I decided not to elaborate.

Stanley and Hazel seemed pleased by my answer. They even agreed with the part about big cities. It seemed that once Stanley had retired, they moved to a cottage in a small village in Kent, not far from where he had been born and raised. They both admitted to finding it much more to their liking than London.

"London," said Hazel, "has changed – for the worse." Bertie and Stanley nodded in agreement.

To my relief, Bertie did not start his rant about England and London going to hell. Instead he complimented Hazel on a brooch she was wearing – one that, we were told, had belonged to Stanley's great-great grandmother. I have to admit that Bertie, when he wanted, could be charming.

Breakfast that morning was a surprisingly pleasant experience. Stanley and Hazel were delightful. They had to be, I thought, the exception in this country.

After paying the bill and retrieving our luggage, we discovered Stanley and Hazel standing hand-in-hand outside the B&B, admiring the Morris Minor. They admitted to having owned a 1952 model and regretted selling it after a dozen faithful years of service.

Hazel pointed to a shiny but nondescript blue Rover 200 with a "Smiley Face" sticker on the bumper and noted that while the Rover was more comfortable, modern and a whole lot faster, it just didn't have the personality of their dear departed Morris Minor. Stanley agreed. I could only wonder how seemingly intelligent people could actually attribute a "personality" to an inanimate object.

Bertie pointed out what he considered the more prominent features of our Morris Minor: low light headlamps, divided windscreen, something called a "semaphore trafficator," and the ever-popular bumper-widening piece. He mentioned that his father had purchased the car, new, for a grand total of 359 Pounds Sterling. The old couple reacted as if they had been given a private viewing of the Crown jewels.

Bertie suggested that Stanley sit behind the wheel of the antique, an offer he accepted without hesitation. The old man took a seat on the driver's side, his hands resting on the steering wheel. At first he just smiled, then a peculiar look came over his face and I swear I saw the man's lower lip quiver. Obviously overcome with emotion, Stanley sat there for a few more minutes staring into space and wiping the tears from his eyes. When he got out he and Hazel hugged both Bertie and me.

As I pulled away from the B&B and drove the Morris Minor onto the highway, I glanced at the rear view mirror. The old couple was still standing there, waving us goodbye.

Stanley's arm was around Hazel, and he had a bittersweet smile on his face. It was my guess that Stanley was watching his past, his lost youth, motoring off into the distance. I knew how he felt. I took a sidelong glance at Bertie. He had removed his glasses and was wiping a tear from his eye.

I waited a few minutes before asking Bertie my standard question. "Okay, Bertie, what's our destination today?"

"Today, my good man, we visit the lovely village of Little Longcote. We continue due west on A272, and I would estimate a time of arrival of about 2 p.m. Of course, that all depends on how many pubs we visit on the way."

"Fine, but do you think we can spend a little less time in each pub, Bertie? Can't we just show the drunks the print and ask them flat out if they have ever seen the church or not? Yesterday we only were able to hit three pubs."

"Vince, you can't just walk in and walk out. If you want people to take us seriously, and to have any interest at all in what we're looking for, you first have to get them on your side. That takes a little talk, and at least one pint."

"Okay, chat them up if you must, but could you make it just a half-pint?" I asked.

Bertie looked horrified. "Vince, a *man* doesn't order a *half-pint*."

My first reaction was that the English were way too much work. Giving the matter more thought I finally decided that, while I hated to admit it, Bertie was probably right. My in-your-face approach had gotten me absolutely nowhere. Bertie's technique had not gotten us much further, at least in terms of finding the church, but at least he was able to motivate everyone in the pub to help out.

"By the way, Vince," Bertie added, "just because a bloke has a pint or two in a pub doesn't make him a drunk."

The drive to Little Longcote was uneventful. The countryside, however, was gorgeous. I really had no idea that this little island had such beautiful scenery – or so damn many birds.

We were able to stop in two pubs and one fast food franchise eatery on the way. Bertie was adamantly opposed to the stop at the restaurant, but I needed a hamburger fix and thought that we might find someone who could point us to the church. Unfortunately, the hamburger tasted like wet straw, and the people inside were mostly French and German tourists. In any event, we still hadn't found a soul who admitted to ever having seen our little church.

We arrived at Little Longcote at about 4 p.m. and managed to locate a promising looking B&B. After moving the luggage to our rooms, Bertie suggested the same old routine. I should drive about in mindless circles while he explored the local pubs. He seemed in an inordinate hurry to hit the first pub of the evening. I decided to make myself a cup of coffee in the room before venturing out. The day of driving, coupled with the hard bench seat of the Morris Minor, had caught up with me and the level of pain was substantially more than usual.

Finishing the coffee, I decided against driving aimlessly around the outskirts of the town. It hadn't made much sense the first time Bertie suggested it, and it made even less now. Instead I decided to visit the large church in the village square. After all, if one wants to find a particular church wouldn't it make sense to talk to the local vicar? Well, at the time it seemed like a good idea.

I left the B&B and walked to the square. The house of worship there was a Church of England franchise, and I hoped that I could find the vicar in the small, ivy-covered cottage next to it. As I walked to the cottage I happened to glance at the graveyard at the rear of the church. A familiar figure was standing there, his back to me. What in the hell, I thought, was Bertie doing in a graveyard? After a moment of apparent reflection, Bertie bent down, removed his glasses, and appeared to be reading the inscription on one of the tombstones. There were flowers on the grave and it looked fresh. I stopped and watched.

Bertie straightened up, put his glasses back on, and stood very still for a moment or two. Then he removed his cap and hurled it at the grave marker. He followed this with a string of expletives. Until then I didn't know that the man had such a rich, colorful vocabulary. Clearly, Cousin Bertie was sorely vexed. Even more clearly the little weasel had an enormous amount of explaining to do.

Bertie bent over, picked up his cap, and turned toward me. His pale face got a shade or two paler. He walked toward me, stammering and gesturing, making no sense whatsoever. When he was within about ten feet he stopped, composed himself, and said, "Vince, I suppose you wonder what that was all about?"

"You're damn right, Bertie. I want some straight answers, and I want them now."

Bertie nodded and pointed to a bench. We sat down, neither one of us saying anything for a few minutes. Bertie finally broke the silence.

"Vince, you're not going to like what I have to tell you. But hear me out. Maybe you'll be able to understand."

I refused to answer or look at him.

Bertie sighed. "Vince, I want just as bad as you to find a final resting place for Jenny. But there's something else I want, and I'm afraid I've been using you – and Jenny – to help me with that matter." He paused, waiting for a response. I fixed my stare on the First World War marker in the center of the village square.

"All right then, here's the story. Let me finish before you do anything rash."

I maintained my silence. That produced an even deeper sigh from Cousin Bertie.

"When Mum was sick, really sick, she agreed to be admitted to hospital. That was about three months before she died. I visited her every day, and everyday there was this other chap there, visiting his mother. We got to talking and he told me that he was from Lower Friththingden, that little village we visited on Saturday." Bertie paused, waiting for a response.

I continued to stare at the marker. For such a small village, there were an awful lot of names on it.

"He was the very same chap, Tom Hawkes, that you found me chatting with in the *Errant Hun*. But I'm getting ahead of myself. Tom found out that I have a passion for military history, and he shared some personal military history with me in our chats at the hospital. Vince, he told me that when he was a young boy an American B17 crash-landed in the pasture directly behind the farmhouse he lived in with his mother. It was on the 22nd of December 1943. Tom was sick and in bed. He said he heard a tremendous explosion; an explosion caused by a one-ton German parachute mine. The very same explosion that destroyed the *Sow and Centipede* – the pub that was rebuilt as the *Errant Hun*."

Bertie looked at me for a response. I continued to stare at the marker. There were thirty-seven names on it.

"Young Tom looked out his bedroom window and saw a plane crash-land; like I said, it was an American B17, a Flying Fortress. He saw five Yanks get out of the wreckage, one with a bandage around his head. His mother took the men into their farmhouse. Right about then two Rolls-Royce motorcars – Phantom IIIs mind you – drove into Tom's back garden and a bunch of men jumped out. Tom watched as long as he could and then lay back in bed, falling asleep and not waking until the next day. And, Vince, do you know what his mother told him?"

Not getting an answer, Bertie continued. "His mum told him that the plane he saw crash-land wasn't American; it was German. She told him that there were no survivors, and she told him to *never* talk about the event again. She made him swear that he would not. That day they took the wreckage away. Tom says that the American markings had been painted over, but that he knew it was, absolutely, a B17."

I had to admit that the story was mildly interesting. "Bertie, just why should I give a shit about this story?"

"Vince, please, let me finish. You'll understand then."

"Okay, go ahead and finish. But I really don't know why you should give a damn about a sick little boy who imagined that a B17 crashed in his back yard."

"He didn't imagine it, Vince. That's why it's so interesting." Bertie reached into his inside jacket pocket and pulled out a manila envelope. He opened it and handed me a faded photograph.

"Tom took photographs that day. Later on, he developed them himself. This is one of them," said Bertie "Only three people in the world have ever seen this picture, you, me, and Tom."

"All right, I can see a plane, clearly in pieces – and a group of men with their backs to the camera, standing by the plane's wreckage. What of it? I would imagine that there were a lot of planes crashing into the English countryside during the war."

"Look closely, Vince. Look closely. See the markings on that plane? They're American. And, look at the shorter man – the one in the bowler hat. Notice anything familiar about him?"

I squinted at the photo once more. "Are you going to tell me that the chubby little guy with his back to the camera and wearing the bowler is Winston Churchill?"

"That's exactly what I'm going to tell you. If that's not Churchill then it's someone who looks a whole lot like him, at least from the rear. And look at those motorcars. Those are Rolls-Royce Phantom IIIs, just like Tom said. Not exactly the type of motorcar you would expect in your back garden."

"All right, let's assume for the moment that the guy in the photo is Churchill. What of it?"

"Vince, remember that I told you that Tom's mother claimed that the plane was German, and there were no survivors?"

"Yeah, and again, what of it?"

"Well, Tom insists he saw five Yanks. One, with the bandaged head, dropped something in the grass. Tom found it the next day." Once again Bertie reached into his inside jacket pocket, this time pulling out a tin of tobacco. It looked like the same tin that Tom Hawkes had handed him during our visit to the *Errant Hun*.

Bertie opened the tin, turned it over, and something fell onto his open hand. Shit, it looked like a mummified human ear!

"This," said Bertie, "is what the Yank dropped. Evidently his ear was sliced off; how I don't know. But this is definitely an ear. Wouldn't you agree?"

"I agree, now put that ghastly thing back in your tin. But, Bertie, if this is so then it would mean that Tom's mother lied to him. Why?"

"Tom didn't find that out until years later, when his mum was admitted to hospital. It seems that she had been told to never tell anyone about the Yanks. Part of the group that had been in the Rolls-Royce motorcars told her she mustn't tell a soul, that it was vital to the war effort, that she never, ever talk about the incident. It wasn't until she knew she was about to die that she finally told Tom the truth."

"So, was Churchill one of the guys who talked with her?"

"Tom's mother said that some of the men remained outside, and that she never got a good look at that part of the group. But she believed that one of them was Churchill."

"Why? Why Churchill? What in God's name is Winston Churchill doing in a backwater village like Lower Friththingden a few days before Christmas, in the middle of a war? Wouldn't you think he had better things to do?"

"Rumor had it that Churchill had an illegitimate child by a young lady in London. Some say he sent her to Lower Friththingden to have the child. She stayed there for years, never working but able to afford nice clothes and a nice house. The night that the parachute mine destroyed the *Sow and Centipede* it was said that Churchill and his entourage were parked near the village church, listening to the children inside singing Christmas Carols. One of those children was, according to local gossip, Churchill's illegitimate daughter."

"I'm still not getting this. Let's say Tom's story is true. How is it that a German parachute mine lands on the pub on the same night that an American B17 crash-lands outside the very same village? Isn't that just a bit unusual?"

"Yes, it definitely is odd, but odd things do happen in a war. Tom, himself, has never figured it out. But, according to his story – and his mother's – that's exactly what happened. Who knows, perhaps the German plane shot down the B17."

"All right, I can see that someone like you would have an interest in this story, true or not. But what the hell have you been doing since then? Bertie, I saw you coming out of a cottage in Haywards Heath when you should have been visiting pubs and trying to locate Jenny's church. Tonight I see you screaming at a grave marker. Just what's going on?"

"I was just about to get to that. Here's the hard part, Vince. Tom's story piqued my interest. I did as much research as I could on any B17s that were lost on 22 December 1943. There were twenty-three of them. All but one was shot down over France or Germany. All but one was accounted for. The only plane that has never been accounted for is the *Susan Rae*, a Flying Fortress that the U.S. Army Air Corps claimed crashed into the channel – with no survivors, and no bodies recovered."

"And you think that the plane Tom saw is that plane?"

Bertie handed me the photo again. "Look at the tail numbers on that plane, Vince. What do you see?"

"Well, I read 2299. Looks like there may have been one or two more numbers after that, but the tail section appears to have a large chunk shot out of it."

"The first four numbers of the tail number of the B17 that was supposedly lost at sea on 22 December – the *Susan Rae* – were 2299. Vince, this has to be the same plane. It's just way too much of a coincidence otherwise."

"Sounds plausible. But you still haven't explained about your visit to the cottage in Haywards Heath, and your graveyard antics tonight."

"Vince, I'm convinced that the five Yanks are still in England. For years there have been rumors of a so-called American village in England – a place where a number of American deserters located. They say that the village looks exactly like small town America, back in the forties. They've got soda fountains, jukeboxes, and the children even play American baseball. Vince, I don't think it's a rumor. I think the story of the five Yanks and the rumors of the American village all fit together."

Bertie paused, tried to judge my reaction, and then continued. "Tom Hawkes gave me the name of a distant relative in Haywards Heath who lived in the cottage you saw me leave from. The fellow who lived there the past fifty or so years, name of Bill Baldwin, was assigned to guard an enclosed lorry, from Lower Friththingden to Southampton. It was the night of the 22nd of December 1943."

"The same day the B17 crash-landed?" I asked.

"The very same day. According to the story Bill told me, the guard detail was advised that there were five *Canadians* in the lorry, and that they had been in contact with some sort of biological agents – 'deadly germs' he said – and that the Canadians were extremely contagious. The guard detail was ordered to accompany the lorry but to not open the back, or even speak to the men inside."

"And you think the five Canadians were really five Americans?"

"Exactly. Bill told me that, once they arrived at Southampton, they handed off the guard duty to another group. By chance he recognized one of the men in that group, a chap named David Hardcastle – who happened to be a school chum of Bill's. Bill said that he hadn't seen or heard from this Hardcastle chap in years, but he did have his address. That's why we stopped here. I was hoping to talk to

David Hardcastle, to find out where they took the Yanks. I went to the address and met his wife. She informed me that David died – just last week. That's his grave, over there," he said, pointing in the direction of the church, "that I was visiting. Can you imagine that? Just last week."

Bertie didn't say anything for a few minutes, and then continued, his voice now a mournful croak. "Vince, I hit the proverbial dead end." He went silent again.

"Bertie, you miserable little bastard. Do you mean to tell me that we've been driving all over England looking for five American flyers – from the Second World War? And for some silly rumor of an American village? What in God's name were you thinking?"

Bertie sighed. "Yes, that's what I'm telling you. Only I'm afraid it gets even worse."

"How the hell could it get any worse?"

"Vince, about Jenny's church …"

"Yes?"

"Vince, there is no church. The truth is that Jenny's family and mine never went anywhere on holiday except Westcliff-on-Sea, a little resort no more than twenty-five miles from London. Every year, every summer, the same place. Until my time at Oxford, that was the farthest I had ever been outside London."

"But Jenny said her mother painted that church."

"Yes, and she did – on one of our holidays at Westcliff-on-Sea. Jenny and I would play on the beach and Aunt Emma would set up an easel and paint. She painted unicorns, pigs with wings, fairies, angels, and all sorts of fantasies. Aunt Emma had a wonderful imagination. Jenny and I would ask her to paint scenes and she would oblige. That's all the painting of the church is, Vince, something out of Aunt Emma's imagination. Something to please two small children."

"You're telling me that there isn't any church? That we wasted the past few days looking for some mythical American village?"

"I'm afraid so," Bertie replied, his eyes downcast.

I could feel the pain in my lower back increase in severity, nearly taking my breath away. I sat there, trying to focus on the marker in the square, trying not to faint.

"Vince, I can't tell you how sorry I am. It seemed like a good idea at the time. I thought that, with your help, I could find the five Yanks and the American village. I thought that, since Jenny's church doesn't exist, there was no real harm in what I was doing. I'm sure that all Jenny wanted was to be buried in England, and I would imagine that any village church would do. I was going to tell you, honestly. I just wanted to find the Yanks first."

A wave of pain, much worse than anything I had ever encountered, suddenly struck. For a moment I felt that I was about to faint.

"Vince, do you hear me? Vince, what's the matter?"

The pain was so intense I couldn't respond. It had never been this bad, never.

"Vince, you look terrible. What can I do?"

I took a deep breath and answered. "Bertie, just help me back to the B&B."

"Are you sure you don't want a doctor?"

"No, damn it. Just help me up, and then help me back to the B&B. We'll talk about this later. Right now I need to get back and chug down some medicine. Do you understand?"

Bertie nodded and helped me to my feet. Leaning against him, we made our way slowly back to the B&B. Once in my room I retrieved my painkillers, took them without water, and collapsed on the bed. Bertie stood in the doorway, looking like a lost sheep.

"Get out of here, Bertie, and close the door behind you." He hesitated, about to say something, thought better of it and left. That night was the worst I had ever experienced. The shit, as they say, was hitting the fan.

8
TUESDAY, 22 APRIL 1997:
DESTINATION, PORT ISAAC

I was unable to get any sleep the entire night, although the intensity of the pain did subside somewhat a few hours before sunrise. When morning finally came I sat up slowly, my head spinning, and gingerly placed one leg after the other over the edge of the bed. Once the room stopped moving I stood up and walked, a bit unsteadily, to my suitcase. I found what I was looking for in an inside pocket, a well-worn flyer describing the alleged wonders of England's Cornwall coast. On the back of the flyer were directions to the town of Port Isaac, in Jenny's familiar handwriting.

I dressed without either first washing or shaving. Just the effort of putting on my shoes was almost more than I could handle. Once the ordeal of dressing was finished, I packed my suitcase and opened the bedroom door. Using the hallway wall as a support, I made my way to Bertie's room and knocked on his door.

Bertie opened the door. He too was fully dressed. "Vince, how are you?" he said, his eyes growing wide, a grim look replacing his usual morning smile.

"Still alive, Bertie, still alive. Get that suitcase packed and let's get out of here."

"Without breakfast?" Bertie asked.

"Without any damned breakfast. Once you pack your suitcase, go to my room and grab mine – and Jenny's urn.

Don't think I can manage carrying those this morning. I'll be waiting in the car."

I paid my bill and walked, still unsteadily, to the car. I paused for a moment at the driver's side door, thought better of it and got in on the passenger side.

A few minutes later there was a tap on the passenger-side car window. Bertie was standing outside, a look of abject terror on his face. I rolled down the window.

"Bertie, get in on the other side. Today, *old chap*, you drive."

Bertie placed the suitcases and urn in the boot and then walked, like a man on his way to the gallows, to the driver's side and got in. "Vince, I haven't driven a car in over thirty years. I don't have a license. To be honest, I don't think I can handle this."

"I don't really give a damn, Bertie. You've taken me on a wild goose chase all over this miserable excuse for a country. Today, you drive and I'll give directions. You owe me, Cousin Bertie. You owe me. Understood?"

"But, Vince …"

"No buts, Bertie. Turn that key and get this piece of crap on the road."

Bertie stared at the steering wheel for a good thirty seconds before placing the key in the ignition. His hand was trembling, but he finally managed to turn the key. The little sewing machine engine started without hesitation. By then Bertie was sweating like a man about to meet his maker. He looked at me, his mouth forming a wordless question.

"We take A361 to M5, and then head south. Now get the damn car on the road."

We pulled away from the parking spot at a snail's pace. Bertie entered the highway and we crawled away from the B&B. At this rate it would take us days to get to Cornwall.

"Damn it, Bertie, faster! You're only doing ten miles an hour. Move this car!"

After some more encouragement Bertie had the Morris Minor at what appeared to be its upper limit, a shade above 68 mph. The little engine was no longer humming. Instead a dull roar came from the engine compartment. Sweat was now rolling down Bertie's forehead, his face, his chin, and his neck.

"Vince, just where are we going?"

"We're going, my lying friend, to a village in Cornwall. A lovely little place called Port Isaac."

"But why? Why don't we drive back to London? You really need to see a doctor. You look awful. Besides, why in the world do you want to go to Cornwall?"

"Personal business, Bertie. Personal business. Now, do me a favor and shut up."

Bertie drove on without a further word of protest. I reached in my shirt pocket and pulled out two painkillers. I swallowed both, and then leaned back in the seat. All I could hope for was that we would be able to reach Port Isaac in time.

I must have dozed off. When I opened my eyes we had stopped at a petrol station. Bertie was still seated behind the wheel, but he was now shaking violently.

"What happened? Why did you stop? Do we need petrol? Shit, Bertie, get a hold on yourself and answer me."

"Sorry, Vince. Like I said, this is the first time in more than thirty years that I've been behind the wheel of a motorcar. To make matters worse, as I told you this particular motorcar holds some unpleasant memories."

"I understand, but for God's sake man, calm down and get us back on the road."

"I can't," said Bertie.

"Yes you can, you deceitful little ferret. Get this car on the road."

"Vince, it's the motorcar. It overheated. There was steam pouring from the bonnet before I pulled into this station."

"So, your 'reliable' piece of English-manufactured tin has broken down. Isn't that just great? Get off your duff and see if someone inside this gas, excuse me, petrol station knows how to fix the problem."

Bertie got out of the car, found a particularly greasy looking fellow inside the petrol station, and the pair walked back to the car. The guy, a dead ringer for Stan Laurel, looked at the car, whistled, and shook his head. I gathered up my strength and got out of the car.

"Aren't you even going to look at the engine?" I asked the attendant.

"What good would it do?" he replied. "We've got no parts for a motorcar this age. I'd advise you to call the Double A and get this antique moved." With that he turned on his heel and walked back to the station.

"Bertie, open the bonnet on this thing. Let's see if we can figure out what's wrong."

Bertie did as directed. Once the bonnet was open the reason for the overheating was obvious. The fan belt on the tiny engine had split and was now laying on the engine block. I grabbed the remains and walked to the station. After about a half an hour of searching, and with absolutely no help or encouragement from the surly attendant, we were able to find a belt that came close to fitting the Morris Minor. A little on the loose side, but tight enough, I hoped, to get us to the next large town and a more suitable replacement.

With the temporary replacement belt installed, we motored back on to the highway, Bertie again, reluctantly, at the helm.

"Bertie, we'll stop in Exeter. It should be big enough to have an automotive parts store that has a proper replacement belt. We'll spend the night there, but I want to be back on the road again tomorrow, early. Let's find a hotel in the center of town; no B&Bs for tonight." He nodded. All the fight had gone out of Cousin Bertie.

Bertie drove into the center of town, and we found a large hotel, the *Royal*. There was a Pay-and-Display lot behind the hotel, and Bertie parked the Morris Minor in an empty spot near the hotel entrance. My attention, however, was drawn to a car one row over – a very familiar looking car.

"Bertie, look at that blue car over there, the one with the smiley face sticker on the bumper. That looks like Stanley and Hazel's car."

"You're right, Vince. I do believe that is their motorcar. They did say that they were motoring to Exeter for their reunion. My word, they must be staying here."

If I had felt better I would have enjoyed seeing the old couple again. As it was, all I wanted to do was get a room and lie down.

With Bertie's help I managed to make it to the lobby and register. The receptionist gave us a worried look as I walked toward the elevator, leaning against Bertie.

As I leaned against the wall, waiting for the elevator, I could hear the sound of singing coming, evidently, from a nearby reception room. It was the awful "White Cliffs of Dover." Thankfully the elevator quickly made its appearance and we were able to escape the inane doggerel of what has to be, next to "Rudolph the Red-Nosed Reindeer," the world's silliest song.

The room was nondescript, seedy, and small – a typical British 4-star hotel. The much cheaper B&B's we had stayed in were, by far, more attractive. However, at this point in time all I wanted was a bed to lie on, and the lumpy object in the small room would have to do for the night.

"Vince, do you want me to help you off with your clothes?"

That was the very last thing I wanted. "No, just help me with my jacket and shoes. I just want to get into that bed."

Bertie's hands were shaking as he untied my shoelaces. If I wasn't so damn mad at him I might have felt sorry for the man. He was clearly traumatized. I suppose I would have felt the same way, had I been in his place.

#####

I woke to the touch of Jenny's hand on my brow. "Jenny, please help me. Give me the strength to make it to Port Isaac."

The voice that replied wasn't Jenny's. I opened my eyes and saw Hazel, sitting by the bed, her hand stroking my forehead. Standing behind her were Bertie and Stanley, both looking very worried.

"Hello, Hazel. Hello, Stanley. How long have you been here?" I asked.

"Not long. Bertie found us and told us about your problem. I was a nurse, a long, long time ago, and decided to look in on you," said Hazel.

"Hazel, there's nothing you can do for me. There's nothing anyone can do for me. I'm pretty much finished. All I want to do now is to get to Port Isaac. I'm sure that, if I can just rest here a while, I'll be able to get back the strength I need to make it there."

"Bertie told us that you had your heart set on Port Isaac. Do you want to tell us why?" said Hazel, her hand now holding mine.

"I'd rather not," I replied.

"I'm sorry; I shouldn't be such a busybody. Vince, we'll help you get to Port Isaac if Stanley has to drive you there, himself. But you do need to rest, and this hotel is not the place for that. Do you think you have the strength to make it downstairs?"

"With Bertie's help, I'm sure I can. But where are we going?"

"To a dear friend's house. She lives on the edge of town. She, in fact, is the person hosting our reunion this year."

Bertie chimed in. "Vince, Hazel's here to attend a reunion of her nursing friends – an RAF Nursing unit. They all worked together, during the war."

That was a surprise. I had guessed, when we met Stanley and Hazel, that the reunion they were attending was for retired doormen. Instead, it was Hazel's gala event of the year.

I don't recall much of anything of the walk downstairs, or the drive. I do remember that I was sitting in the front of the blue Rover, and that we ultimately drove into the driveway of a large, white Victorian house, surrounded by rose bushes. An old woman met us at the door and led us to a bedroom, the room in which I was to spend most of the next four days.

9
THURSDAY, 24 APRIL 1997:
THE HOUSE OF DIANA BROOKS

I woke to the sound of a woman humming. Opening my eyes I saw that Hazel was sitting in a rocking chair beside my bed, reading. She looked up and smiled when she realized I was awake.

"Good morning, Vince," she said, removing her reading glasses.

"Good morning, Hazel. I do hope you haven't been sitting there all night."

"No, luv, Stanley stood watch last night. He returned to the hotel this morning and brought me back for my turn. Actually, luv, that was the second night Stanley watched over you. Today's Thursday, and you arrived Tuesday."

"Thursday? Good heavens, the last thing I remember is the drive from the hotel, on Tuesday."

"Well, I'm not surprised you don't remember Wednesday. You slept through that entire day."

"Hazel, you have all been much too kind. I simply haven't the words to express my appreciation."

"Vince, you can show your appreciation by just getting better. How do you feel this morning?"

"A little better," I replied. "But, Hazel, I have to admit that I feel tired, more tired than I have ever felt in my life."

"Bertie tells us you've been taking painkillers — lots of painkillers." She reached over to the nightstand and pulled several bottles of medicine from my ditty bag. "I hope that you don't mind, but Diana and I have been looking through your store of medicine. I must say it's a worrisome lot."

"Who's Diana?" I asked.

"Diana Brooks. She owns this house, and is hosting our reunion. I believe I told you, back at the hotel, that we were in the nursing corps together – although I'm not too sure how much you recall about Tuesday. Anyway, Diana may be 'just a nurse,' but she knows more about medicine than any doctor I've ever known."

"And what do you and Diana think of my medicine?"

"We're both wondering why you're taking this particular collection. Diana has an idea, but why don't you tell me? Of course, you are free to tell me that it's all none of my business. Please realize, dear boy, that I'm just concerned for your well-being. We're all concerned."

I saw no point in keeping matters to myself any longer. I explained my situation to Hazel. I told her about the trips to the hospital, the treatments, the disappointments, and the pain. "Hazel, nothing worked. I'm no longer in remission. I was told that I had at most perhaps three or four months to live. That was almost two months ago. They told me there was no hope."

"I'm sorry, Vince. I'm truly sorry."

"It took me a while but I've come to accept it – well, at least most of the time. There's nothing that can be done about it. All I really want now is to get to Port Isaac."

Hazel reached over and placed her hand on mine. "I told Diana that you wanted desperately to go to Port Isaac. She thinks she knows why." At that moment the bedroom door opened and the owner of the house walked in. Tall, slim, and elegant, Diana looked considerably younger than her eighty-four years.

"Good morning, Vince," said Diana.

I sat up in bed, my back resting against the headboard. The effort made me dizzy. "Good morning, Mrs. Brooks. I want to thank you for letting me stay here. You've been very kind. I can't tell you how grateful I am to both you and Hazel … and Stanley."

"Please, my dear boy, call me Diana. As Hazel told you, I have my suspicions as to why you are in such a rush to get to Port Isaac. Tell me, Vince, have you been there before?"

"No, never, but my wife visited there several times with one of her school chums. Her friend, Mary, lives – as I recall – in a town named Truro, evidently not that far from Port Isaac. Those visits were some years ago. Jenny, my wife, said it was possibly the most beautiful place in England. She told me that the two of us would have to go there someday."

"Oh yes, it's quite lovely – and very lonely. They have high, sheer cliffs there. Would that be the attraction?" said Diana.

"Yes, definitely," I replied. Hazel's eyes widened.

"Vince, do you really think that is the best thing to do?" said Hazel, evidently understanding my intent.

"I do. Let me explain; has Bertie told you about the church? The one where I wanted to bury my late wife's ashes?"

"Yes," said Hazel. "Bertie has told Stanley and me everything. He's sick about what he's put you through."

"He should be, but that's no longer my concern. Since the church I was searching for was just a fantasy, and since I haven't got much more time, I want to finish matters … at Port Isaac. *Now*. Ladies, I'm just too tired to go on. It's that simple."

"Vince," said Hazel, "if that's what you want then that's what you will have to do. We're not here to talk you out of it." Diana nodded in agreement. "But you are certainly in no shape to drive anywhere, even as a passenger, much less all the way to Port Isaac. Get some rest and I assure you that my Stanley will drive you there."

"Ladies, give me a half dozen of my painkillers and I'll be fit to drive to the moon, right now."

Diana gave me a stern look and picked up the half-empty bottle of acetaminophen-codeine. "How many of these have you been taking a day?" she asked.

"I started those last week, and I've been taking them regularly ever since I arrived at Gatwick. I'd guess I've been taking four to six pills a day."

"Vince," said Diana, "if you keep taking that many pills a day you'll not live to see Port Isaac."

"What do you mean? I'm not a hero, ladies; I have to admit that I just can't tolerate much more of this pain. What choice do I really have?"

"You have choices," said Diana. "We can talk about those later. Continuing taking those pills, however, is not an option I would recommend if you have business in Port Isaac. My advice is to stop taking those pills. I'll give you aspirin, plenty of aspirin."

"Aspirin?" I replied, shocked to think that, in this day and age anyone would recommend aspirin for my illness.

"Yes, my boy, aspirin. Few side effects and it will cut the pain, at least for now – and it won't make you dizzy and tired. Aspirin and plenty of water will give you some relief. I think that, with another day or two off those painkillers, you may be able to make your trip, if that's what you really want. But right now you simply have to rest and allow time for the medicine to leave your system. That's precisely what I want you to do, and that's an order," said Diana, her mouth a firm line.

I was in no condition to argue. "Where's Bertie?" I asked, immediately wondering why I should care. Yet, somehow – to my surprise, I realized I missed his presence.

"He's back at the hotel, with Stanley. They're taking care of the repairs on the Morris Minor," said Hazel. "Bertie's very concerned about you, Vince. But he's also too ashamed to face you. I do think he really cares for you. Despite his foolish actions he's a good man."

"You're right, I have to admit that Bertie is basically a decent guy," I replied.

"Yes," Hazel continued, "and the two of you have so much in common."

"Hazel, other than Jenny, I can't see that Bertie and I have *anything* in common."

"Oh, but you're wrong there," said Hazel. Diana sat down at the foot of the bed, listening intently. "Vince," Hazel continued, "Stanley and I had a long talk with Bertie yesterday. He told us about you, about your disappointments. About your obsession."

"What on earth are you talking about?" I asked.

"Evidently your wife confided in her cousin. She told Bertie that you had one great goal in life, to be remembered, to be famous, and you spent most every waking hour trying to make that come true. Bertie said that your one great fear was that no one would remember that you even existed. That evidently terrified you more than death itself."

"Ladies, I never realized that she talked to anyone about that," I replied. "Yes, I suppose that was once my fear. At one time I thought I was a pretty hotshot mathematician. I had written lots of papers, lots of books, but there was no real lasting contribution, at least nothing on the order necessary to be a truly famous mathematician."

"Yes, that's what Bertie told us," said Hazel.

"Did he tell you that I came within a whisker of achieving my goal?"

"No, that he did not tell us," Hazel replied.

"The whole story is that I worked, for almost two decades, on the development of a new method for solving a certain type of problem – a problem everyone said was unsolvable. A few years ago I made a breakthrough. My graduate student and I began writing a paper summarizing the development. There was no doubt in my mind that this paper would make me a household world … at least in the world of mathematicians."

The memories came flooding back. "That was about the time that Jenny, my wife, became ill. I took a leave of absence from university to take care of her. For the first time in my professional life I took a break from my research – mathematics were, in fact, the last thing on my mind. It wasn't until after Jenny's death that I found out what had happened to my discovery."

"What was that, Vince?" asked Diana.

"The Mathematics department head threatened my graduate student with flunking out of the program unless she 'cooperated' with him. The paper on my work had already been accepted when I found that out. The paper was ultimately published … without my name on it, not even an acknowledgement. By that time I was ill, much too ill to fight the system. It was my one great discovery, and no one will ever know."

"That's terrible," said Hazel. "But it only proves that you and Bertie have so very much in common."

"Are you going to tell me that Bertie got his life's work ripped off?" I replied.

"In a manner or speaking, yes; that's very much what happened to Bertie," said Hazel.

"I'm not sure I follow you, Hazel."

"Vince, according to Bertie, thirty years ago he felt he had his whole life ahead of him. He was a student at Oxford, a history major. He wanted to go into politics; he even dreamed of being Prime Minister. But then, as you know, there was that terrible accident. Bertie's mother blamed him for the death of his father, and for making her an invalid. He was overwhelmed with guilt."

"That I didn't know," I said, remembering just how little anyone cared for Aunt Fiona.

"She blamed him, and he began to blame himself. He spent almost thirty years trying to make it up to his mother, but she never relented. Even on her death bed she reminded him of his terrible deed."

"She was not a nice woman," I said, understating the case.

"No, she was not. Did you know, Vince, that she could walk?" said Hazel.

"Aunt Fiona? Walk? No way. After the accident she spent her entire life in bed. You must be mistaken."

"No," continued Hazel, "Bertie said she could walk. A few years ago Bertie left his news agency during working hours to return to their flat. He had forgotten his wallet. He found his mother, seated on the couch, reading a magazine. When he had left her that morning, she had been in bed. He believes that she had been able to walk for years."

"So, Cousin Bertie thinks his mother robbed him of his life? I guess I can understand that," I replied.

"Yes, that's essentially what he thinks. This trip with you was, in his mind, quite possibly his one last chance to do something with his life. He felt that, if he could find his so-called American village, and the five Yanks from the Second World War, he could say he had achieved something of importance," said Hazel.

Diana interjected. "What's this about an *American* village?"

"Bertie's obsession;" I replied, "he's convinced that there's a village, somewhere in England, full of Americans. Or, at least, five particular Americans. He claims that this American village is a virtual replica of a small town in America, from the forties, complete with hot dogs, hamburgers, juke boxes, and bobby socks."

"Very interesting," said Diana. "Please tell me more."

I told her everything I knew. The story of Tom Hawkes, the photos he had taken, the ear in the tobacco tin, Bertie's frantic search through the South of England, and how he had reached a truly dead end in Little Longcote.

"Vince," said Diana, "there are a number of legends – stories about both Americans and Germans who were shot down over England, and then disappeared into the countryside, never to be seen again. There's even one tale of five Americans, survivors of a B17 crash, who were taken to a small village, where supposedly they live to this day."

"Right," I replied. "That's the tale that Bertie seems to believe."

Diana nodded and continued. "Some say that the Americans went 'native,' becoming even more English than the English. Some say that they turned the English village into an American village – just as Bertie seems to believe – where everything is exactly as it was in America, fifty years ago. Others say that these stories are nonsense."

"I'd have to agree with those who say they're nonsense." I replied.

"Oh, would you? Then, my dear boy, you just might be wrong," said Diana.

"What are you talking about?" I asked. "Don't tell me that you believe that fairy tale."

"Vince, in – as I recall - either January or February of 1944 I was asked to assist a physician, Dr. William Jones-Sinclair, on a mission that was to be kept absolutely confidential. We were driven from London to Devon, not far from Great Torrington. There we were placed in the back of a military lorry. There were no windows; we weren't able to see where we were being driven. It was all quite mysterious."

Drawing a breath, Diana continued. "We were taken to a small military camp, nothing more than a collection of rude barracks really. We stopped at a building that served as the field hospital. We were allowed out of the lorry, but told not to visit any of the other buildings. Inside there was but one patient, a young man. He was very ill, suffering from pneumonia."

"An American?" I asked.

"We were simply told that he was a 'soldier,'" Diana replied, "and that he had been part of a secret mission. There was no mention of his nationality. We were asked to help the man, to cure him if at all possible. We were sworn to secrecy."

"Go on," I said, my interest piqued.

"There was another man, a man I never spoke to – a tall, skinny fellow. He would stand outside the field hospital for hours on end. He would just stand there, in the cold, and stare at the building. I did notice that he had no insignia, badges, or any indication of rank on his clothing, and I found that strange. I was later told that he and the sick man were best friends."

"You said this other fellow was tall. Did you happen to notice if he was missing an ear?" I asked.

At first Diana seemed taken aback by my question. Then a thoughtful look came over her face.

"No, I never noticed a missing ear. But, when I think back, I do recall that he was always wearing a cap – one with earflaps. If memory serves me, I do believe that those earflaps were always down," said Diana.

"Ah," I said, "interesting. What about the other fellow, the sick one? What happened to him?"

"The man lived, but it was nip and tuck. The doctor stayed with him during the day; I stayed by his bedside every night. It was clearly very vital – to someone, someone very important – that this man live. That first night his fever got worse. He was delirious and started talking about his wife, and how she had cheated on him. He said something quite strange about having 'painted her over.' On other occasions he would rave on about the Yankees and Indians; I believe he was talking about American baseball. Vince, this man said he was one of five survivors of a B17 named the *Susan Rae*. In fact, he said he was the pilot."

"My God, Diana, that's the name of the plane that Bertie has talked about. And one of the survivors was said to be tall, and missing an ear – I'm betting he was the tall, skinny guy who waited outside the hospital. This means that the story is true. Those fellows actually exist."

"No, it's not quite that simple. After hearing your story I'm now quite sure that the five Americans were, indeed, all living in those barracks at the time we visited. A few months after the war, however, Dr. Jones-Sinclair called me. He wanted to inform me that the men that had been stationed in the barracks had all returned to the front, a few months after our visit. He said that someone in the Ministry of Defence had just informed him that the men had been killed in action. I found his call rather strange. A number of the men that I had cared for during the war had returned to the front, and some had likely been killed there, but no one in the Ministry of Defence had ever felt it important enough to let me know."

"It certainly sounds like someone in the government wanted to make sure that you thought the five Americans were dead," I said.

"I agree," replied Diana. "Of course, after more than fifty years, they could all be dead now – of old age."

"Diana, do you have any idea where that military base is, or was?" I asked.

"It so happens that I have a very good idea. My fiancé was from Devon. When we were young we would walk the footpaths there. I may not know the exact position, but I do have an idea as to the approximate location. But let's talk about that later. I'll bring you a cup of tea. After you drink that I want you to rest. It's going to take a while to get those painkillers out of your system."

Diana and Hazel left the room, leaving me with my thoughts. I spent the rest of the day thinking about the five Americans. When Diana brought me dinner that evening, I made a request.

"Diana. Would you do me one more favor?"

"That depends on the favor," she replied.

"Don't tell Bertie about the five Americans."

"Do you really think it's fair not to tell him? After all, according to Hazel he's spent a great deal of time and energy looking for the Americans, and his American village."

"No, I agree it would not be fair to not tell him. But I want to be the one to do so."

"All right then, I'll not say a word."

10
FRIDAY, 25 APRIL 1997:
DIANA'S DIRECTIONS

By Friday afternoon some of my strength had returned, and – best of all – the pain had lessened considerably. Diana encouraged me to get out of bed once every two hours and walk for at least ten minutes. The first few times I tried I was quite sure I couldn't even make it across the room. By that evening I was feeling well enough to walk downstairs.

Strolling through Diana's house was like visiting a museum. Sepia and black and white photos were on every wall, mantel, coffee table, and anywhere else they could conceivably be placed. Most were of a young man and young woman. The young man was in a military uniform, the RAF. The young woman was stunning; she had one of the most beautiful faces I have ever seen.

I asked Diana about the young couple. As I suspected, the woman was Diana. Most of the photos had been taken in the early to mid nineteen-thirties. The man was Diana's fiancé. He died in a plane crash just two weeks before their scheduled wedding. She ultimately married another man, a wealthy banker named Clarence Brooks. But she informed me that she had, upon Clarence's death, burned every photo of him, along with all his clothing and belongings. Judging from the fire in her eyes, I decided not to pursue that matter. She did say that it was after her husband's death that she became a nurse.

I was about to ask her about her experiences in the war when she suddenly changed the subject.

"Stanley and Hazel will be having dinner with us. Perhaps you'd like to take a bath and get dressed? Do you feel up to that?"

"Certainly," I replied. "But what about Bertie? Won't he be joining us?"

"Hazel tells me that Bertie inquires about you on a regular basis, but still doesn't want to face you. From what I've been told, you were rather hard on that poor man."

"I would have to agree; it was not my proudest moment. At the time I thought Bertie deserved to be drawn and quartered. Now, I can only say that I am deeply embarrassed. But I do intend to make it up to him."

"The five Yanks?"

"That's right. The five Yanks. Which reminds me, would you ask Stanley and Hazel to bring an ordnance survey map of Devon to dinner tonight? But not just any map. Have them bring one of Bertie's maps. Ask them to make sure it's the oldest version he has, in case he has more than one map of Devon. They're in book boxes, in the rear seat of Bertie's old Morris Minor."

"I'll tell them. But what's so special about Bertie's maps? I have a Michelin's map of England in my study. It's really quite good, and only a year or so old."

"My guess is that Bertie's maps are from the forties, or perhaps earlier. We're looking for a military installation from that time. A lot has changed since then. I think we need the older maps."

#####

Stanley and Hazel arrived at precisely half past seven. They had indeed brought the ordnance survey maps with them. However, it was agreed to leave that matter until after dinner.

Stanley and Hazel said that I looked infinitely better than on Tuesday. Hazel was convinced that stopping the painkillers had made the difference. Diana made no comment on that observation. Whatever the cause, I was just glad that I felt stronger. The pain was there, but I decided it was something I could tolerate – at least for now.

I found that the more time I spent with Stanley and Hazel, the more I liked them. They were kind, funny, and genuinely concerned about my health. Diana too was someone very special. I felt very fortunate to have met these three wonderful people. I only wished that it could have been under different circumstances.

Finishing dinner, we retired to Diana's parlor for brandy – although I was only permitted tea. It was only then that the subject of Bertie, and the maps, was brought up.

"Vince," said Stanley, "we've brought the maps you wanted. I must admit that Bertie was quite baffled by that request."

"Can you convince Bertie to come by tomorrow morning? I'd like for the two of us to get back on the road again."

"You're not going to force that poor man to drive again, are you?" said Stanley. "Vince, he told us he hadn't driven a motorcar in nearly thirty years. The poor chap doesn't even have a license!"

"I'm not sure. It all depends on how I feel. If need be, I'll ask Bertie to drive. He's really not that bad a driver. Considering everything, he did very well."

"Well," said Stanley, "we'll do what we can to convince him to come by in the morning. Vince, he really does want to see you. It's just that he feels his treatment of you was inexcusable. He's terribly embarrassed. I can tell you that the man is truly sorry."

"That's in the past. Tell him that … tell Bertie I miss his ugly mug, and that I want very much to continue our journey."

"He'll not come if he thinks you might be wanting to travel to Port Isaac," said Hazel.

"You can tell him that I won't ask him to do that. That I can promise. Now, might we take a look at his maps?" I asked. Stanley reached for the ordnance survey maps and placed them on the coffee table.

I examined the maps and picked one dated pre-Second World War. I passed it to Diana, who was seated next to me on the couch. "Diana, do you think you can pinpoint the location of that military installation you visited?"

Diana thumbed through the pages until she reached a particular one. "Here's a likely suspect," she said, pointing at a large expanse of land labeled simply "Danger." "Typically, when you see something marked like that you can be reasonably assured that it is a military installation – quite possibly a place with lots of unexploded bombs and ammunition."

"Diana," I asked, "any guess as to where in that Danger zone those military barracks you visited might have been located?"

"No, I'm afraid not. But isn't this good enough? You now have a good idea as to the general location, don't you?"

"Possibly, but the area you identified must cover a good hundred square miles. It would be helpful if we could pinpoint it just a little closer," I replied.

Hazel chimed in. "These maps show all sorts of landmarks. Look at the upper right-hand side of this page. It even indicates that there was an ancient iron-age settlement there at one time. Do you remember any landmarks at all, Diana?"

Diana closed her eyes and appeared to go into a trance. For a good ten seconds no one in the room said anything. She finally opened her eyes, a look of excitement on her face. "Yes, I do remember one thing. The barracks were surrounded by a thick forest but, if you looked down the road – the single-track dirt road leading away from the barracks –

toward the west, I seem to recall that there was a folly on the next hillside, perhaps two or three miles distant."

"What's a folly, Diana?" I asked.

"They're buildings, constructed for no other purpose than to satisfy the whims of some wealthy landowner. Most tend to be brick or stone towers. Often they're made to look ancient, although most are from the 18th or 19th Century. As I recall, the one that could be seen from the barracks was of limestone. In the afternoon sunlight it looked like a tower of gold," said Diana.

Stanley pointed at the map. "Would that be it?" he said, his finger resting under a position on the map labeled simply, "folly."

Diana examined the map closely. "It could be. It certainly does sit west of the region labeled 'Danger'. Yes, this just might be the place."

Shortly after 10 p.m. I asked to be excused. I was tired, yet excited. Stanley and Hazel assured me they would absolutely insist that Bertie drop by tomorrow morning – after he had breakfast with them at the hotel. I was counting on it.

Before retiring I took a quick peek into my ditty bag. All the medicines were there, including the painkillers. I closed the bag, reached for the bottle of aspirins, and took two. I followed those with a large glass of water. I had placed my confidence in Diana.

11
SATURDAY MORNING, 26 APRIL 1997:
TWO TABLESPOONS OF MARMITE

The night went relatively well. I did swallow two more aspirins at around 2 a.m., however – as Diana had assured me – the pain was bearable. I also was less tired and felt that I was thinking more clearly. When morning came, I was able to wash, shave and dress without having to sit down and rest. Finished, I checked my wristwatch. It was 8:30 a.m. Bertie should be around in an hour or two. In the meantime I would break bread with Diana, a woman whom I was beginning to greatly admire.

I could smell the aroma of a full English breakfast as I made my way down the stairs. Either I had grown used to it, or Diana's offering was less offensive than most of the versions I had sampled previously. I did, however, pass on Diana's offer of Marmite. Diana looked at me disapprovingly.

"Vince," she said, "I'd like you to do me a favor."

"Anything, Diana. You've been wonderful – I can never repay you for your kindness. Tell me what you want and consider it done."

"My dear boy, I want you to eat at least two tablespoons of Marmite each day," she replied.

I couldn't believe my ears. Was Diana joking? The look on her face indicated she was serious.

"Two tablespoons of that ghastly stuff?" I asked, pointing at the Marmite jar in disbelief. "What on earth for?"

"It's a superb source of Thiamine, Riboflavin, Niacin, Folic Acid, and Vitamin B12. You may not like its taste, smell, or appearance, but it should improve your stamina. Vince, we gave it to our RAF personnel during the war, and it did wonders for them. Besides, you already promised me." She passed an unopened jar of Marmite to me, smiling much too smugly.

"All right, a promise is a promise."

"Then you might as well start now. Try some Marmite on a piece of toast. Here, use this jar," she said, handing me the one she had been using. "Keep the unopened one for your trip."

I opened the cap on the jar. The smell was just awful. I took a butter knife and dabbed a glob of Marmite on a piece of toast. Gathering my courage, I bit into the toast. It tasted even worse then it smelled. Diana watched me intently, a hint of a smile on her face.

I was left with no choice. I held my nose and ate the rest of the toast and Marmite just as quickly as I could. Diana had, by then, dissolved into giggles.

Once she stopped laughing, her expression became serious. "Vince, I have something else for you." She reached under the table, bringing up a small white box with a red cross on it.

"There will come a time when the pain will increase to a point where aspirins will do no good. When that time comes, I would recommend that you use this," Diana said, pointing at the medical kit. "I can assure you that it is preferable to leaping off a cliff."

"Thank you," was all that I could think to say. She simply nodded.

#####

Shortly before 10 a.m. I heard the sound of a car turning into Diana's gravel driveway. Glancing out of the front window I saw Hazel in her blue Rover. Following close behind was Bertie's Morris Minor, even shinier than usual. Stanley was at the wheel of the antique, beaming like a kid left alone in a candy store. Bertie, on the other hand, sat stoically in the passenger side seat, looking as if he were about to walk the last mile.

"Diana, you've got company. Hazel, Stanley, and Bertie just arrived."

"Oh good," said Diana from the kitchen, "do open the door and welcome them. I'll be there as soon as I get this apron off."

I followed orders and opened the door, to be greeted warmly by Hazel and Stanley. Bertie stood to the rear of the old couple, looking for all the world like a whipped puppy.

Bertie gave me a quick glance and then looked at the floor. "Lo, Vince, must say that you are looking much better than when we brought you to Diana's." Hazel and Stanley nodded in agreement. Diana, emerging from the kitchen, graced us with her Mona Lisa smile.

"I have you all to thank for that. You've been much too kind. I'm really sorry to have caused so much trouble," I said.

"No trouble at all, young man," said Diana. "We only wish that your stay could have been under more pleasant conditions."

"We are all agreed on that," said Hazel. "But Stanley and I are going to have to say our goodbyes. The reunion was a grand success, thanks to Diana, and now we've got to be on our way."

First Stanley and then Hazel gave me a big hug. I realized that I was sincerely going to miss these two. I hadn't cried for years, not even when Jenny died, but I felt myself on the verge of tears. It was a troubling and mystifying experience. How, I wondered, could two people, strangers but a few days ago, make such an indelible impression?

We went outside and waved the old couple goodbye. As their blue Rover disappeared into the distance I turned to

Bertie. Tears were streaming down his face and he removed his glasses to brush them away. Surprisingly, he didn't seem at all embarrassed.

Diana ushered Bertie and me into the parlor, and then excused herself. There were now no distractions. It was just the two of us, once again. Bertie, sitting on the couch, seemed resigned to his fate.

"Bertie, I want to apologize for my behavior," I began. Bertie's eyes widened. This was clearly not the dialogue he had expected.

"And I want to make it up to you. I believe that your birthday is three weeks off, and I'd like to give you an early birthday present."

Bertie looked absolutely befuddled. "A birthday present? For me? My word, Vince, how did you even know my birthday?"

"That's easy, Bertie. Your birthday is exactly three weeks after Jenny's. Today is Jenny's birthday, so yours is three weeks off. Every year she would start looking for a present and card for you on the very day after her birthday. That was her signal to shop for her cousin. Jenny picked out the card and present, but I was always the one who mailed it."

"I appreciate the thought, Vince, but I really don't deserve a present. After what I did to you what I really deserve is a punch in the snoot."

"Bertie, tempting as that offer is, I'd prefer to give you a much better present to remember me by, certainly one a little less violent."

"I appreciate that, Vince, particularly your refusal to punch me. So, my friend, where is this present?"

"It's about a day's drive from here. Bertie, my friend, you and I have a beautiful day for a drive. Why don't we get on with it?"

A frown came over Bertie's face. "Vince, I'll not be going with you if the destination is Port Isaac. That's a trip you'll have to take on your own. I'll be no part of it."

"No, Bertie, we'll not be traveling to Port Isaac. Don't worry about that. We're off to finish your quest."

'My quest? Are you talking about the American village? About the five Yanks?"

"Precisely. But this time *I've* planned out the route. You drive and I'll give directions."

"Vince, you know that I shouldn't be driving. For one thing I don't have a license."

"I'll pay any fines you might incur. I'd drive but, frankly, I'm really not up to it yet. Let's do this, Bertie, you and me. I want to meet those five Yanks, and I really want to see the American village. I've also got an idea as to where to bury Jenny's ashes. Let's you and I just find a quiet, peaceful church in a nice little village and make that her final resting place. I really think that's all she wanted. So, are you up to it?"

"All right, I'll drive. But, first, just what have you learned about the whereabouts of the American village? How in the world do you know where it is?"

"Help me with my suitcase and the urn. Let's get the car packed, and I'll tell you on the way."

We finished packing the Morris Minor and then said our goodbyes to Diana. I was surprised, once again, by the emotions I experienced. I realized that I was truly going to miss this wonderful and classy lady.

We left Diana and the town of Exeter at about 11 a.m. Bertie, looking somewhat more comfortable in the driver's seat, piloted the Morris Minor through the center of town and back onto the motorway. Unlike our previous drive, he actually seemed to be enjoying himself.

"Bertie, before I answer your questions about the American village, let me ask you something. What, my friend, do you intend to do once we find the village?"

"That's easy, Vince. I'm going to sell my story to *Hello! Magazine*. I'm guessing that they'll pay plenty for this story. Of course, we'll split that."

"Bertie, no need to split the pot. For one thing, this is *your* quest, and you did all the hard work. I just happened to get lucky. For another, I'm really not going to need any money where I'm going."

"I wish you wouldn't say that, Vince. Miracles, you know, do happen."

"Well, if that miracle does happen, all I'd like from you is this automobile. How's that?"

"The Morris Minor? You can certainly have it but I've got to admit that I haven't been under the impression that you cared much for this motorcar."

"I guess it's grown on me. I have to admit that this little car is just as tough and reliable as you promised. Besides, the only thing that has gone wrong has been the broken fan belt – and, as I recall, that was a Japanese product."

Bertie gave me a big grin. "Vince, once we sell the story you will be the proud owner of this fine motorcar. Besides, I'm thinking that I'd like to buy a sports car, perhaps a Ferrari. Of course, I first need to get a license."

"A Ferrari? Did I hear you right? Bertie, the fellow who dislikes all things foreign, is going to buy an *Italian* car?" Bertie's only response was a chuckle.

Over the next several miles I told Bertie about my discussions with Diana, of her long ago trip to the barracks that she believed housed the five Americans. Bertie shook his head in amazement.

I picked up the old ordnance survey map and pointed to the place where it was assumed Diana had visited. Bertie pulled off to the side of the road and asked to examine the old map more closely.

"So, this is why you wanted my maps of Devon. My word, this is remarkable. Vince, the gods are smiling on us."

"You can say that again," I replied. If we hadn't met Stanley and Hazel, and if our fan belt hadn't broken, we would have never known." Bertie nodded in agreement.

"But you mustn't get your hopes too high, Bertie. It's been more than fifty years since Diana tended that one ill American. It would seem inconceivable that, even if any of the B17 survivors are still alive, they would still be residing in those old barracks."

"Agreed. But at least we're back on the trail. Who knows, if our luck holds out we may find clues as to where they went after their stay in the barracks. Even if we never find them, we still may get enough evidence to sell the story."

"There's one other thing, Bertie. Diana said that, shortly after her visit to the barracks, she was told that all five of the Americans had returned to the front. She was told that they were all killed in action. Both she and I agreed that the story might have been a ruse, used to throw people off track. But it's something else we need to consider."

"Vince, whatever the case, let's just focus for now on finding those barracks. That in itself would certainly be enough to make my day."

"I've got my fingers crossed," I replied.

"Me too," said Bertie, "but now let's take a look at some of my other maps." With that he exited the parked car and retrieved one of the book boxes.

"What are you looking for?" I asked.

"I've got a mix of old and new ordnance maps in here, Vince. I'd like to see a more recent map of Devon. Things have changed, as you might guess, since those old pre-War maps were made."

Bertie soon found what he was looking for, an ordnance survey map of Devon no more than a few years old. He handed the map to me.

I showed Bertie the approximate page and position on the newer map of our destination. Tugging at his chin, Bertie examined the map – in excruciating detail.

"See anything of interest?" I asked.

"I do, Vince, I do. See the area marked 'Danger,' the region where Diana said the barracks are located? Notice that there's a bit of a difference between that region on the two maps."

"Well, it does appear that the Danger zone is somewhat larger on the newer map. Other than that, it doesn't look as if much has changed in that area over the past fifty or so years."

"I would have to disagree," said Bertie. "Look at those two villages on the southern edge of the Danger zone on the old map, the ones nearest the main road. Then take a look at the new map."

"They're gone! It looks as if the Danger zone was extended, and that those two villages simply disappeared. Interesting, but what difference does that make? We're just looking for the barracks."

"I'm not sure if it makes any difference, Vince. But it would seem to indicate that the military installation has grown over the years. That means it may still be active, and that means we might have some trouble gaining access."

"Bertie, at this point in time there is nothing that is going to stop me from finding those barracks, even if I have to cut through a fence and sneak onto the land."

"I'm with you there, Vince, but we probably need to be prepared. Let's stop at the next village and buy those wire cutters you seem so desperate to use. We might also want to pick up a few other things."

"Like what?" I replied.

"Can't say I'm sure about that. I have to admit that this will be the first time I've ever done anything like this. Let's just find a hardware DIY store and try to guess at what we'll need."

Sometime later we entered a mid-sized village. Bertie immediately spotted a hardware store, an ironmonger establishment of surprisingly large size for so small a place. He parked in front of the store, remarking that it might well be the only hardware store left between here and our aptly named destination, the Danger zone.

We entered the store and scoured it for any items we felt might be of use. We wound up with wire cutters, a collapsible shovel, a small axe, and a burlap bag. I found a large pocket knife having – in addition to a standard knife blade – a spoon, a fork, and a bottle opener, and added that to our purchase. The owner gave us a funny look when Bertie asked, half jokingly, about night vision goggles, but he rang up the sale and we managed to pack everything in the boot of the Morris Minor.

Bertie suggested that we have lunch at a pub across the street. Despite my aversion to pubs, I agreed as it was past lunchtime and I was feeling hungry. First, though, I asked for the keys to the car and retrieved the jar of Marmite that Diana had given me.

"Vince, is that a jar of Marmite that you have there?" The look on Bertie's face wavered between amazement and bemusement.

"That's right, Bertie. And I don't want to hear any cracks about it."

The pub was nearly full but we managed to order two Ploughman's lunches – Bertie's with a pint of bitter, mine with lemonade – and find the only empty table left in the establishment.

"Bertie, you wouldn't happen to know how many teaspoons there are to a tablespoon, would you?"

"I believe three, Vince. Why do you ask?"

"You'll see," I replied, pulling out my new knife.

When the food arrived I opened the Marmite and, using the spoon on my knife, quickly swallowed six teaspoons of the awful stuff, followed by a swig of lemonade. Bertie's eyes went wide but he didn't ask any questions. I didn't offer any explanation. It was just too much fun watching Bertie's response to my new diet supplement.

By the time lunch was over Bertie had made friends with most of the people at the surrounding tables. When we left the pub and got back into the car I decided to ask him, straight out, a question that I had been pondering the entire trip.

"Bertie, I don't mean anything personal – this is just plain old curiosity – but I have to admit that I remember you as being the world's biggest bore. Again, nothing personal, but I recall people crossing the street just to avoid talking to you on my previous visits. But now you seem to be the life of the party wherever you go. I guess what I'm trying to say is, just what the hell happened?"

Bertie chuckled. "Vince, you're quite right. I was certainly a tiresome human being. It wasn't until about twenty years ago that I finally had to face up to that. Do you remember the elderly twin sisters you met when we left London, the Devlin sisters?"

"Yes, I do. Sweet old ladies as I recall."

"Nothing at all sweet about the Devlin sisters, Vince. Those two are hard as nails, and they can drink any man under the table. When the local pub was still open the three of us were regular customers. We used to sit at our usual table, in the corner of the pub, and I would entertain them with my stories. At least I thought I was entertaining them."

"What do you mean?" I asked.

"Well, one day I had a sore throat. Could barely get a word out. The Devlin sisters and I sat at the table, drinking away, not a word being said. After about a half hour Sara Devlin looked me in the eye and asked me why I wasn't talking. I croaked out a response; told them I had a sore throat. They just looked at me. So I got out a pencil and wrote them a note on a napkin. Do you know what the two of them did then?"

"Haven't got a clue, Bertie."

"They both took off their glasses. They had hearing aids attached to them. Then they both turned on the hearing aids and started gabbing amongst themselves. You can't imagine how I felt. Come to find out they had been doing that for years, turning off their hearing aids whenever they were in my company. Until that day I never realized it."

"You drank with those ladies, for years, and never realized they weren't listening to you? That's remarkable ... and funny."

"Well now I can look back on it and see the humor in the situation. But, let me tell you, I was devastated then. I didn't go back to the pub for two weeks – and, when I did, I decided to ask the Devlin sisters about the matter."

"What did they tell you?"

"They told me that they hadn't wanted to be rude and move to another table, or to avoid me. They even said that they felt sorry for me, and were quite sure that no one else in the pub would want to have me sit at their table. They agreed, however, that they would have gone quite mad if they hadn't turned off their hearing aids."

"I'm afraid I know just how they must have felt," I replied. "So what did you do next?"

"I apologized. Told them how sorry I was, and promised that, from then on, I'd let them do the talking."

"I assume that satisfied them?"

"No, it did not. They told me that I'd have to learn how to talk *to* people, instead of talking *at* them. It made me think. It made me wonder why I acted that way around people. It made me wonder what was wrong with me."

"And your conclusion was?"

"Vince, I think I was just trying way too hard. My mum made me feel like I had murdered my father, and crippled her ... and that it was all my fault. All my plans for the future had been dashed by that accident. I felt worthless, and I guess I just wanted other people to know that I wasn't totally useless. To be truthful, I guess I wanted desperately to impress on people that, although I may be nothing more than a newsagent, I was still smarter than them. That's pretty sad, don't you think?"

"I suppose so. I just wish I had taken the time to understand you a long time ago. Do you know that Hazel told me, just this Thursday, that you and I have a lot in common?"

"She said that?" Bertie replied.

"Yes, she was referring to the fact that we were both 'obsessed.' You with finding the American village, and me with being famous. However, I'm afraid that we have more in common than just that. We just dealt with the matter in different ways."

"What ways? What matter?" asked Bertie.

"I've had lots of time to think things over the past few days. I came to the conclusion that we both wanted to impress people. You took the course of boring them to death with your knowledge of trivia. I, on the other hand, just cut off contact with people. I stayed aloof, unapproachable. Other than Jenny, I've got to admit that I have no real friends."

"That's not true, Vince. I'm your friend. I didn't feel that way until very recently, I must admit, but I would hope that you now consider me a friend."

"Bertie, I would be honored to have you as a friend, and I hope the feeling is mutual."

"It most definitely is. So, Vince, as a friend, might I give you some friendly advice?"

"Certainly," I replied, wondering just what was coming next.

"Okay, here goes … but feel free to tell me to shut up at anytime. Vince, the two of us definitely handled our problems poorly, and that's probably the understatement of the century. I'm hoping that I've managed to improve the way in which I deal with the world, but you need to give some thought as to what you might do."

"Go ahead. What's your advice?"

"My advice, for whatever it may be worth, is to loosen up. You, my friend, are what is known as a tight ass. You're stiff and, as even you admitted, condescending. Vince, you never make small talk. I've watched you in some of the pubs we visited. You just walk up to people and ask them about the church. No small talk, no introduction. You acted as if you didn't give a damn about them. All you wanted was for them to give you a prompt answer." Bertie looked over at me for my reaction, and then continued. "Vince, are you ready for me to shut up yet?"

"No, go right ahead. What you're saying is true. But how do I change, Bertie? How, after years of being a 'tight ass' and insensitive oaf do I suddenly change? How did you change?"

"Vince, it took a while. It's not something you manage overnight. Lord, I can't tell you how many self-help books I read on the topic. It was months before I finally decided that the answer wasn't in any book. It had to be in here," said Bertie, pointing to his heart.

"You've lost me."

"What I mean is that you can't think this through; you have to feel it," Bertie replied.

"Sorry, Bertie, but that sounds way too touchy-feely. I'm a scientist, and scientists can't *feel* that something is right, they have to *prove* it."

"Let me put it another way, a way a mathematician like you might understand. Dealing with life is just not something you can put into an equation and solve for the correct answer. Vince, you can't over-think it; you just have to give up and recognize one crucial thing."

"And that one crucial thing is?" I asked.

"That everyone is pretty much the same. If we're at all normal, we want people to like us, to notice us, and to respect us. It's pretty much the Golden Rule, Vince, all you really have to do is treat people the way you'd like to be treated."

"Sounds way too easy," I replied, shaking my head.

"Oh, but it isn't at all easy, particularly for the likes of you and me. You can't just walk around complimenting people and telling them what you think they want to hear. I tried that, and I can tell you it doesn't work. They soon think you're just an insincere lout. Vince, you've got to really mean it. That, my friend, takes time and practice."

"Practice?" I asked. "I'm afraid that you've lost me again."

"Vince, what I finally did was to try to pretend that whoever I was talking to was *me*. I knew how much I wanted to have people talk to me, to compliment me, and to like me. So I just assumed that they felt the same way and that it was my duty to make them feel like they were important. Most of all, I had to want to do all this for *their* sake, not mine."

"And it worked?"

"Not at first. At first I tried too hard. After a while though, it became more natural. Sort of like playing Cricket."

"Like Cricket? If that's the case, I'll never be able to change. That game makes no sense at all to me." I replied.

"What I mean is that in a sport, like Cricket, it takes time before things become natural. At first you're thinking about your batting stance, and all the coaching you've ever received. But, after you practice enough, it becomes natural. You don't have to think about it anymore, and you're a much better player. It's the same with meeting people. It takes practice, but *if* you really care it will become natural."

"Okay, maybe I can do that. But first, how do you come up with something about an absolute stranger that would make him feel important?"

"You keep your eyes and ears open. First of all, you engage the person in small talk. If you're observant, you'll soon find something special about that person."

"Lord, Bertie, I've never been able to make small talk."

"Vince, I have to tell you that comes as no surprise. You come across as if you don't have time to waste on small talk. You're much too impatient. People interpret that to mean that you really don't want to waste your time on them. Frankly, Vince, you scare the hell out of people."

"I'll give small talk a try," I replied, meaning it.

"Good, but realize that you and I have been making small talk for quite a while. That wasn't all that difficult, was it?" Bertie replied.

"I suppose you're right. Like I said, I'll give it a try. I promise. But there's one other question I'd like to have answered. It's something that has been bothering me this entire trip."

"What's that, Vince?"

"You've treated me different than everyone else we've met on this trip; at least up until today. You've not bored them to death with a lot of trivia. But with me, it's been a different story. Why's that?"

"You're right, Vince. I reverted back to my old ways with you. To be frank, I just felt so uncomfortable around you that I felt compelled to babble, to talk about anything and everything. That's over. Things will be fine from here on, I can assure you."

"I understand, Bertie, and I promise not to make you uncomfortable. Or, at least I'm sure going to try. But, to be honest, I do have to admit that some of your stories are actually interesting. In fact, once in a while you do come up with some amazing bits of trivia. I guess what I'm trying to say is that, should you feel compelled, I'd like to hear the occasional story – just as long as it has nothing to do with birds."

Bertie chuckled. "Agreed. An occasional bit of trivia will be served up, subject to anything regarding avian wildlife being strictly off limits."

12

SATURDAY AFTERNOON, 26 APRIL 1997: THE "DANGER" ZONE

It was nearly four in the afternoon when we arrived at a point near the site of the Danger zone. Immediately before the turnoff leading to the military installation, Bertie parked the car on the side of the road and we traipsed up a nearby hill, to – as Bertie insisted – get the lay of the land. I had to stop a few times to catch my breath but managed to reach the top of the hill where Bertie stood, scanning the countryside.

"See any Indians, General Custer?" I asked.

Bertie ignored the sarcasm. "What landmarks should we be looking for?" he asked.

"According to the map, that side road there, the one about ten yards in front of the car, might – if we're lucky - lead to the barracks. The only landmark that I know of is a folly. Diana said that it was a tower, and that it glowed like gold in the evening sun."

"I can't see any tower, Vince. Nothing but hills, grass and trees."

"Perhaps it's hidden by the trees, or the hills. Why don't we just head down that side road and see if we come across it – or the road leading to the barracks?"

We trudged back to the car and headed down the narrow side road.

"Bertie, did you notice that there were no signs at the intersection of this road with the main road? Isn't that a bit odd?"

"It is. Up until now there have been signs at every little cow path we've crossed but you're right, there weren't any signs at that intersection. Perhaps the army doesn't care to draw attention to the fact that there's a military installation in this area."

Roughly two miles down the side road we came to another unmarked intersection and encountered the first car we had seen since turning onto the road.

"Look at that, Vince, that's a brand new Land Rover, Defender 90 series, in British Racing Green. Quite an impressive motorcar, don't you think?"

"Bertie, for a guy who hasn't driven in thirty years you sure know your automobiles. Yeah, it's quite a car, but I still prefer your Morris Minor."

"Me too," said Bertie, rather unconvincingly. "But say, did you get a look at that chap driving the Range Rover? Big, burly fellow. Did you notice the look he gave us when we passed?"

"More like a glare," I replied.

We drove on for about three miles before spotting the folly. Just as Diana had said, it looked like an ancient tower. Constructed of yellow limestone blocks, I would imagine it would glimmer like gold at sunset. The road to the barracks should be directly across from the tower, but try as we might, we found no sign of any road leading east.

"Bertie, it's been more than fifty years since Diana was here. Perhaps the road is just no more. Who knows, it might have been ploughed over years ago. Maybe we should drive back to the folly and park the car there. We can then walk, directly east, across that meadow and into the forest on the hill there."

"Are you sure you don't want to wait in the car, Vince? You may be overdoing it."

"I can make it. Besides, I wouldn't want to miss this for the world."

Bertie drove back to the folly and parked the Morris Minor in a lay-by. We opened the boot and took out what we thought we might need – the collapsible shovel, the burlap bag, and the wire cutters. Closing the boot, we walked across the road and into the meadow. I tried not to show it but I was tiring fast, my heart pounding in my chest and the pain in my back increasing.

"Bertie, you go on ahead. I don't want to slow you down. I'll be with you directly."

Bertie walked ahead and I brought up the rear. Every few minutes or so I'd stop, open the collapsible shovel, and lean on it. When I finally reached the thick grove of trees I began to wonder how I would find Bertie.

I entered the forest and attempted to continue on a due east course. If Diana was right, the barracks were in that direction. I soon came to a wire fence, with a sign proclaiming "DANGER, Unexploded Ordnance." Directly below the sign a small hole in the fence, just big enough to fit Cousin Bertie, had been cut. I crawled through and continued my trek.

After about ten minutes I entered a clearing. There, standing forlornly, was Bertie.

"What's the matter, Bertie?" I asked.

"Look around you, Vince. There were certainly buildings here at one time – you can see the concrete foundations. But that's it, that's all that's left."

"Damn," I replied, "I know we didn't expect to actually run into the Americans, not after all these years, but I was hoping that there would be something here to prove they existed."

"Well, old chap, we've come up empty. Damn is right," said Bertie. "Damn it to hell."

I sat down on a fallen log. Sure enough, just as Bertie said, I could see the concrete foundations of at least a half-dozen buildings. The very faint outline of a road was also evident, the road that Diana must have taken in and out of the area so many years before. I noticed one other thing, a small mound about forty yards behind one of the foundations. It was overgrown with weeds and grass, but it was clearly man-made.

"Bertie, see that mound over there? I'm guessing that's where whoever lived here dumped their garbage. What do you think?"

"You're probably right, but why the sudden interest in garbage?"

"Well, if the Americans dumped their garbage there, then maybe they left some clues. First of all, were the people who were here actually Americans? Second, maybe they left something that will help us figure out where they went. Hell, Bertie, people throw all sorts of things in their garbage."

Bertie frowned, thought it over, and replied. "Okay, let me relieve you of that shovel. After all we've been through I suppose we might as well resort to digging through garbage. You just sit there and rest; I'll see what I can do."

I sat on the log watching Bertie dig into the mound for about five minutes. Feeling a little stronger, I decided to give the surrounding area a closer look.

"Bertie, I'm going to follow that path over there, the one heading east through the woods. Maybe I'll get lucky and find something." Bertie, having removed his tie and sweating profusely, grunted his approval.

The path intrigued me. While the road leading to the barracks was all but gone to weed, the little path through the woods was relatively clear. I had the feeling that people – or possibly animals – were still using it. Walking about half a mile from the site of the barracks I found myself on the crest of a hill, looking down into the loveliest and greenest valley I'd ever seen.

Most of the idyllic landscape appeared to be covered by farmland and pastures. However, on the southern-most edge of the open area I could see buildings, and a river. But it was one particular building that caught my eye. I turned and walked, as fast as I could, back to the barracks.

Just as I was in sight of the area where Bertie had been digging, he gave out a yell. "Vince, come here, look what I've found," he hollered, his voice tinged with excitement.

"I'm coming, Bertie. What's up?" I decided to find out what Bertie had found before showing him my own discovery.

Bertie stood by the opened mound, holding a yellowed newspaper, and pointing to a stack of old newspapers on the ground. "Take a look at these," he said.

As I got closer I could see that he was holding a copy of the sports section of the *Cleveland Plain Dealer*. The date on the paper was Sunday, 13 March of 1944.

"They're all *Cleveland Plain Dealer* papers, Vince, every last one of them. Whoever was living here from about January to early April of 1944 was receiving papers from the States."

I bent down and rummaged through the stack on the ground. "Bertie, have you noticed that these are all *sports* sections from the *Plain Dealer*, and each one from a Sunday edition? There's no other sections, no front sections, no business sections, just sports sections. Did you uncover any other papers?"

"No, those are it. Nothing but the sports sections of the *Cleveland Plain Dealer*. The bloke must have been one keen sports fan, don't you think? And pretty damn important to be receiving papers from the States during a war." Bertie replied.

"Definitely, and the obsession with Cleveland sports jives with something Diana told me. She said that the American she met here raved on about the Yankees and the Indians. Those are American baseball teams. That means that one of the Americans was probably a Cleveland Indians' fan. I'm wondering if he was such a diehard fan that all he read was the sports section?"

"So, you think this proves it was one of the five Yanks?" asked Bertie.

"Well, there's no way to prove it but it certainly adds more credence to our guess that the Americans we've been looking for were here, at least for the first few months of 1944. And I don't believe that story about them returning to the front and all being rather conveniently killed in action. My guess is that they sat out the rest of the war. Who knows, they might have even established that American village of yours right here in Devon."

"I agree, but where do we go from here? Everything else I dug up was just regular old trash, empty cans and such. I found nothing else to prove that the five Yanks were here, and nothing to indicate where they went. All I can say for certain is that they consumed an amazing amount of Spam, and at least one was a fan of Cleveland sports teams," said Bertie.

"Bertie, I don't know where we go from here. But I've got to admit that I overdid it today. I'm tired. But first let me show you what I found, and then let's find a place for the night."

"You found something? What?" asked Bertie, his face brightening.

"I need to show you, Bertie. I think you'll find it interesting. We just need to follow that path over there."

"Are you sure you can make it?" Bertie asked.

"Definitely, this is something I want both of us to see. I can rest later. Just follow me," I replied, walking toward the path.

I stopped at the crest of the hill, pointing out the valley below. Bertie seemed decidedly unimpressed.

"Lovely place, Vince. Lovely," he said, his face showing disappointment.

"Indeed it is, but take a close look at that village over there. See anything familiar?"

Bertie took his glasses off, wiped the lenses, and then replaced them. A few seconds later he locked on. "My word, I see what you mean. That little church yonder looks quite like the church in the painting. My word."

"Right, there's even a brook running alongside. It's like Jenny's painting has come alive. Are you sure that Jenny's mother never ventured this far from London?"

"Vince, as I told you, before moving to the States with Jenny, Aunt Emma lived her entire adult life in London, and I certainly never heard her mention anything about having lived anywhere else but London before she married my uncle. The only trips she made were the yearly holidays at Westcliff-on-Sea. I can't believe she possibly could have ever visited here."

"Perhaps she saw a photograph, or painting of that church, Bertie. How else do you explain it?"

"I can't explain it. I'm guessing though that you'd like to visit that little church. Am I right?"

"You're definitely right. Let's find that village. Perhaps we can even find a place there to bed down for the night."

We trudged back, through the woods, under the fence, and onto the clearing, pausing only once when Bertie thought he had spotted a particularly rare bird. Once on the edge of the clearing we could see the road, and the Morris Minor. However, the old car had company. "Bertie, isn't that the Land Rover we saw back at the intersection?" I said, referring to the green sports utility vehicle now parked behind the Morris Minor.

"I believe it's the same one," said Bertie, a frown crossing his face. "We may be in trouble."

As we walked a few steps farther, the occupant of the Land Rover started his car and drove off, leaving us to ponder the event. By the time I reached our car I was nearly out on my feet. Bertie opened the passenger side door and helped me into the comforting familiarity of the old Morris Minor.

"We'll head directly for the village," said Bertie. "We'll find a place to sleep for the night. You get some rest and tomorrow we'll see what we can do about the church, and Jenny's urn. But, first of all I want to check the map."

Bertie opened the pre-war version of the ordnance survey map and examined it. He then opened up the newer version and compared the two. Judging from the pleased look on his face, he must have found something interesting.

"Vince, I think that village we saw from the hill is this one," he said, pointing at the older map. "It's shown as Withington-in-the-Marsh on the old map, but it is completely missing from the new map. But Withington certainly is to the southeast of where we were. That must be the place where the church is located. If I'm not wrong, I think the intersection we passed – the one where we first saw the Land Rover – should lead to the village center."

"Sounds fine to me, Bertie. Let's go.

13

Bertie drove back to the intersection and turned onto the road where we had first spotted the Land Rover. It was a narrow, rutted, single-track dirt road that didn't really look like it led anywhere except, perhaps, a remote farmhouse. Within a few hundred yards of entering the road, however, it abruptly broadened and changed into a proper paved two-lane roadway.

"Odd, that, don't you think," said Bertie, referring to the change in the road.

"Definitely. It's even odder that there's apparently a village at the end of this road that doesn't appear on any recent maps. What's your guess as to the reason for that?"

"Omitting the village might just be a mistake by the mapmaker. But having this little road change from dirt to macadam is certainly suspicious. I suppose we'll discover the reason once we reach Withington."

We drove for a few more miles before we came to the edge of a village, the same village we had seen from the overlook outside the site of the abandoned military barracks. A small sign proclaimed "AVALON: Please drive carefully." Below that was an even smaller sign that indicated that Avalon was a bird sanctuary.

"Avalon?" said Bertie, his eyes narrowing. "According to the old ordnance survey map this should be Withington-in-the-Marsh. Could they have changed the name of the village, as well as removing it from the map?"

"Bertie, this is just getting stranger and stranger." Bertie nodded in agreement.

The tidy little village of "Avalon" looked to be the home of perhaps two or three hundred people. There were a number of village folks on the sidewalks, each one giving us a look-over. I had the feeling that their interest wasn't confined to the Morris Minor. My guess was that the residents of Avalon didn't see many out-of-towners.

"Vince," said Bertie, "have you noticed the absence of signs on the streets and buildings? The names of the shops are there, but other than that there are no advertisements anywhere. This has to be the most uncluttered village I've ever laid eyes on."

"You're right about that," I replied. "And there's one other thing. There are a lot of young people and children in this little village. In the other villages we passed through I'd guess the average age to be sixty or more."

"I hadn't noticed that until you pointed it out," said Bertie. "I agree, not that many pensioners in Avalon. And note the absence of Nike trainers, fast food restaurants, and souvenir stands."

"And the absence of cars." I added. "I've only seen one other car on the street, and but a half dozen or so parked."

We drove through the village and several back streets but we were unable to find any sign of either a B&B or hotel. Bertie, however, rapidly located what appeared to be the only pub in town, a pub with a rather strange name, at least for England.

"Let's stop in at the *Forest City*," said Bertie. "Perhaps they have a room."

The *Forest City* public house was a two-story, thatched-roof building and, like all the rest of the buildings in the village, constructed of yellow limestone. Its architecture was likely

18th Century and quite pleasing to the eye. It was, in fact, the finest looking pub I had yet encountered.

Although dog-tired, I was able to make it out of the car without assistance, and the two of us entered the pub, hoping for food and lodging. Inside, the pub looked very much like most any other country pub, only perhaps a bit larger and tidier. The walls were adorned with framed black and white photographs of what appeared to be cricket, soccer and rugby players. Judging from their uniforms and facial hair, I'd have to guess that they were players from the early years of the 20th Century.

One surprise was that there was not a single television set in the pub. Of all the pubs we had visited on our quest through the South of England, this was definitely a first.

What really got my attention, however, was the big, muscular looking fellow seated at the end of the bar. I gave Bertie a nudge.

"Bertie, the guy over there looks awfully familiar. Isn't that the man who was driving the green Land Rover, the character who was giving the Morris Minor the once over when we came out of the woods?"

"I believe it is; we do seem to keep bumping into that chap," said Bertie, seemingly unconcerned.

I found a seat at a table near the bar. Bertie, in the meantime, walked to the bar to inquire about a room. The big fellow at the end of the bar gave Bertie a quick glance and then returned to the solemn business of finishing off his beer. If he recognized us, he didn't show it.

"Sorry," said the bartender, a middle-aged fellow who didn't seem particularly happy to see us. "No rooms here. No rooms in the entire village in fact. We don't get many tourists here. Avalon is a bit off the beaten track for that."

"Well, what about some food and drink? My friend and I would like something to eat. Vince," Bertie said, turning to look at me, "what would like for your dinner?"

"I'm not real hungry, Bertie. Just a lemonade would do fine."

"My friend will have a lemonade. I'll have a pint of bitter and a plate of fish and chips, with extra mushy peas if you please." Pausing, Bertie examined a yellowed sign on the wall to the left the bartender. "That sign says that any customer who can put a name to all those pictures hanging on the walls can have a free drink. Does that offer still stand?"

"Certainly," replied the bartender. "But I should tell you that the sign has been there for nearly fifty years, and no one yet has received a drink on the house. If either you or your mate can name those chaps you can both have your drinks free. In fact, I'll even throw in your dinner, a room for the night, and a full English breakfast in the morning." The bartender's offer was met with laughter all around, with the exception of the Land Rover driver who remained expressionless, eyes focused on his pint.

Bertie walked to each picture, with most of the pub's patrons following close behind, and began naming, with an air of absolute certainty, the men in the photos. I didn't recognize a single name, but his answers were met with murmurs of approval. Within a few minutes he had apparently found the correct answer to every picture.

Looking quite pleased with himself, Bertie faced the bartender. "All right, my good man, I believe we are owed drinks, food and lodging." The bartender smirked. The crowd, with the exception of the Land Rover owner, laughed.

"Not quite yet; you have one more picture to go." Moving aside, the bartender pointed to a faded photograph that he had been standing in front of.

Bertie looked at the photograph, scratched his head, tugged his ear and seemed about to surrender. I decided to intervene. There was something very familiar about the face of the man in the photograph. "Just a second, Bertie, I'd like to have a closer look at that picture."

I walked to the bar and took a quick glance at the picture. "That, my good man, would be Tris Speaker."

The bartender looked slightly bewildered and then directed his attention toward the big man at end of the bar. The Land Rover owner, his face expressionless, simply nodded.

"Good Lord," said the bartender, "so the bloke in the picture is named Tris Speaker. Never heard of him. What sport did he play?"

"He was a baseball player," I replied, "for the Cleveland Indians, back in the States. Before my time, but one hell of a player. Got his 3000th hit in 1924 or 5, as I recall."

"The 17th of May, 1925, to be exact," said the big man at the end of the bar. He then stood up and exited the pub. As he closed the door behind him the atmosphere in the pub seemed to change. The tension I had sensed on our arrival seemed to dissipate.

"Gentlemen," said the bartender, "you are the first to ever identify the bloke in that picture. I honestly thought I would go to my grave without ever knowing who that man was. Congratulations. Your food will be ready in a few minutes. I'll personally show you to your room once you're ready." Reaching over the bar, he shook our hands.

Several of the patrons patted Bertie and me on the back as we returned to our table. Others, however, retreated to the back of the room, talking in hushed tones and periodically glancing at us. Our victory had apparently received a mixed reception.

Bertie just sat there staring at me, shaking his head in disbelief. "Vince, how in the world does a mathematician, one with absolutely no time for trivia or small talk, know that the chap in the faded picture over there is that of some obscure American baseball player from the twenties?"

"First of all, Bertie, Tris Speaker is hardly obscure. He may have been before my time, but he's a baseball legend. That's particularly the case if you were born and raised in Cleveland, Ohio. I may be a mathematician, but what I always wanted to be was a baseball player. And there's something else you should know."

"What's that, Vince?"

"I think I just figured out why this pub is named the *Forest City*. The original name of the Cleveland Indians was the *Forest City* team. But what I can't figure out is how our Land Rover driver fits into the picture. He's certainly not old enough to be one of the B17 survivors. But he sure as hell would seem to be a died-in-the-wool Cleveland Indians' fan. Can you believe it, Bertie, he knew to the very day when Speaker got his 3000th hit?"

"My word. My word," was Bertie's only reply.

My dinner that evening consisted of two tablespoons of Marmite, followed by a swig of lemonade, finished off with four aspirins. Afterwards, Eddie the bartender, true to his word, showed us to our room. It was a large room with two twin beds. Both were unusually long, or at least considerably longer than any bed I had yet to run across in England. The bathroom was directly across the hall. Everything was neat and tidy. But it wouldn't have made much difference to me if it had been a pigsty; I was done in for the day.

"Get some rest, Vince," said Bertie. "I'll be back up in a while. I'd like to talk with some of the village folk before I retire. And I think I'll have another pint of the local brew. Got to admit that was the finest pint I believe I've ever had. Brilliant stuff."

14
SUNDAY MORNING, 27 APRIL 1997:
THE VICAR'S STAND-IN

I must have fallen asleep as soon as I hit the bed. I dreamed of baseball, of being in the old lakefront stadium and watching the Cleveland Indians with my father. Only my father looked like Tris Speaker. In fact, everyone around me looked like Tris Speaker.

When I opened my eyes it was morning, and the sunshine was streaming through one of the bedroom windows and into my eyes. Off in the distance I could hear the bells of the village church. I rolled over and saw that Bertie was awake, sitting on the edge of his bed watching me, a look of concern on his face.

"How are you feeling, Vince? That was quite a busy day, yesterday, but you seemed to have slept rather soundly last night."

"I feel surprisingly good. Still a little tired, but all in all I'd say I'm feeling well this morning. Not to worry. So, Bertie, did you learn anything from your time in the pub last night?"

"Possibly. When I asked why the village wasn't on the map the answer I got was that it was simply an omission, and that the villagers all thought it was a good thing. They'd rather go on about their daily lives as they always have than see the village become yet another English country-side tourist trap-*cum*-theme park."

"I suppose that could be the case," I replied. "And I've got to admit that it's refreshing not to be in a village full of pushy tourists, fake Tudor houses, overly quaint tea shops, and hordes of Tee shirt vendors. Not to mention acres of butt-ugly Pay-and-Display lots."

"I agree," said Bertie. "Another thing I found out was the name of the big bloke at the end of the bar, our Land Rover driver and expert on Tris Speaker. He's Walter Kipling and he, or at least his father, used to own the *Forest City* pub. The family is now involved in farming as is, from what I can tell, the majority of the village."

"This Kipling guy, is he an American?"

"I asked about that too. I was told that Walter was born right here in Avalon, some forty or so years ago. However, one of the chaps mentioned that Walter's father, Bobby, was originally from Canada. Interesting, eh?"

"Damn interesting. Both you and Diana said that the British military tried at first to pretend that the five Americans were Canadians. Now we know that Walter's father claims to be a Canadian. Bertie, I've got the feeling that we're close to finding our five Americans. But one thing that bothers me is that this sure isn't the All-American village we thought we'd find. I've got to tell you, I've been in most of our fifty States, and I've never come across any place that looked like this."

"I have to agree. Vince, this village is definitely English. I've not seen one hot dog, one American flag, or even a hint of an American accent. The only thing remotely American was that photograph behind the bar. In fact, when I think about it, this is far and away the most English of the English villages one could imagine."

After washing, shaving, and getting dressed Bertie and I went downstairs to the living quarters behind the bar. Eddie's wife, Martha, greeted us with a weak smile and went about preparing a full English breakfast. It was superb. Either she was an excellent cook or the meal was growing on me. I even had second helpings of the black pudding. I also discovered that it was a lot easier to spread my two tablespoons of Marmite on toast rather than attempt to eat it plain. It also drew considerably less attention.

Eddie seemed somewhat friendlier than yesterday and ultimately peppered us with questions about both London and the United States. I began to wonder if he had ever been outside the village, and decided to find out.

"Eddie, have you ever visited London?" I asked.

"Oh yes. I lived right outside London, Kingsport to be exact, until I met Martha. We met while students, at LSE."

"LSE?" I inquired.

"London School of Economics. We both received degrees there, before getting married. I had intended to find a post in the Finance District, with one of the major banks, until Martha suggested I visit Avalon. After seeing this little village, Martha's birthplace, we both agreed that we'd rather live here. So we moved here and bought the *Forest City*. That was about twenty years ago."

Bertie and I exchanged puzzled looks. I imagine he was thinking the same thing I was: why in the world would two people with degrees in Economics from a prestigious university be running a pub in a little village that wasn't even on any map? Martha must have read my mind.

"Eddie and I are thankful that we didn't get ensnared in the rat race in London. There's no amount of money that could make me ever want to leave Avalon, even with its problems." Eddie nodded in agreement.

"What problems?" asked Bertie. "This little village looks spot on perfect to my eyes."

Martha frowned and looked to Eddie for help.

"Avalon is a lovely place, but that's only on the surface. Unfortunately, the army installation up the road pretty much ruined things," said Eddie.

Looking more and more uncomfortable, Eddie continued. "It seems that the army conducted some experiments, some rather nasty experiments, during the war. Evidently they weren't too careful about the way in which they either stored or got rid of the results. It wasn't until later that the consequences started being felt."

"What consequences?" asked Bertie.

Martha sighed and turned away. Eddie, his eyes downcast, replied. "The land hereabouts is polluted. Polluted beyond repair. What could be the loveliest village in all of England has been ruined. Damn shame. Damn shame."

Eddie shook his head and rose from the table. "I've got work to do, chaps. Need to change clothes. I'm filling in for the vicar this morning." Without further explanation Eddie turned on his heel, leaving the room.

Bertie gave me a worried look – about, I assumed, the pollution. For my part all I could think about was Eddie's odd remark about filling in for the vicar.

When we finished breakfast Bertie and I decided to take an early morning stroll. Our destination was to be the village church, the one we had first seen from the overlook.

The walk through the village was pleasant. The streets themselves were empty and I remarked that the villagers must be either sleeping in or attending church services. Bertie placed his money on them sleeping in.

Along the way I looked for any clues that might suggest that this was the legendary American village. However, other than the faded photograph in the *Forest City* pub, I saw no evidence of anything even remotely American.

Bertie, on the other hand, seemed transfixed by the local trees, stopping here and there to peer into their branches.

"Vince," said Bertie, his face aglow, "I've never seen such a variety of bird life. Look halfway up that oak, on the limb to the right. If I'm not mistaken that's a Mistle Thrush; some call it the Stormcock. Quite a handsome bird, eh?"

"Yes," I agreed. It appeared that Cousin Bertie had found his very own bird Shangri La.

"Odd that such a polluted place attracts these birds. Odd, that," said Bertie.

I nodded in agreement, beginning to wonder if it was such a good idea to bury Jennie's ashes in such a place.

The church lay to the south of the village. A fast running, crystal clear brook flowed between the village and the church, seemingly precisely in the same spot as in Jenny's painting. There was, however, one troubling difference.

"Bertie, those pine trees shouldn't be there."

"What do you mean? What pine trees?" asked Bertie.

"Those three large trees standing between us and the church." I replied. "They come close to completely blocking the view of the church from this vantage point."

Bertie seem more puzzled than ever. I stopped and pointed, through an open area in the trees, toward what little could be seen of the church.

"Bertie, we're looking at the east side of the church, the very same side as in the painting. But the view from here is nearly obscured by those pine trees. Those trees certainly weren't in the painting. If I were going to paint that church I certainly wouldn't set up my easel on this side."

"You're right. I see what you mean. Those are Yew trees, by the way. They're evergreens, and some live to be a thousand years old. That group doesn't appear to be near that old, but they've certainly been here a long time – possibly fifty or sixty years. I have to agree, Vince, it doesn't seem likely that anyone would have chosen this vantage point to paint the church."

"Then we've not found the church in the painting," I replied. "Damn, I really thought this was it."

"Vince, keep in mind that the church in the painting wasn't real. This one is, and this place is certainly beautiful. I think Jenny would be very happy to rest here."

Once again, I'd have to agree that Bertie was right. Jenny would have loved this place, Yew trees or no Yew trees. Again, though, the thought of the pollution concerned me.

Crossing a small wooden bridge we entered the churchyard. From inside could be heard the sound of singing.

Bertie decided to venture inside to look around. I stayed outside, to look for a proper spot to bury Jenny's urn.

For a small village, there were certainly a lot of graves and gravestones, many going back several hundred years. Walking to the rear of the church I found a clustered grouping of more recent graves.

The most impressive of the lot was the gravestone of a Douglas D. W. Stevenson, a gentleman born in 1915 and who had died only last year. The inscription on the gravestone was a poem, one that I remembered from high school.

Under the wide and starry sky,
Dig the grave and let me lie.
Glad did I live and gladly die,
And I laid me down with a will.
This be the verse you grave for me:
Here he lies where he longed to be;
Home is the sailor, home from sea,
And the hunter home from the hill.

It was a Robert Louis Stevenson poem, inscribed on the gravestone of a man named Stevenson. Rather fitting, I thought. Directly below the poem was carved a coat of arms, featuring an eagle, lion, unicorn and songbird of some type, possibly a bluebird.

Bertie joined me as I was examining the graves. He was grinning from ear to ear, and shaking his head.

"Vince, it's quite remarkable. The church is absolutely packed, standing room only. You don't see that sort of attendance in an English church nowadays. But that's just the half of it. More amazing is the fact that Eddie, the proud owner of the local pub, is preaching to the congregation. When he said he was filling in for the vicar, he wasn't joking. Astonishing. But what about you; have you found a proper spot for Jenny?"

"Bertie, this is certainly a lovely place, and the church does resemble the one in the painting. But I'm wondering if it would be right to bury Jenny in a place that's polluted … beyond repair."

"I've been thinking about that too," replied Bertie. "I certainly wouldn't want to live here, but I don't think that's any reason not to bury Jenny here."

"I suppose you're right," I replied. "I guess that I should talk to the village vicar and see what we can do about burying Jenny's ashes. Once that's done, I'd like to stick around here for a while."

"Vince, if you stay, I stay."

"What about your news agency? Your flat back in London? The pollution?" I asked. "There's no reason to risk your shop and your health for me."

"Nigel has made me an offer on the news agency. In fact he's taking care of things in my absence. He's keen to have it, and I'm ready to let go. As far as the flat goes, I'd be pleased to never see it again. As to the pollution, as long as we don't stay overly long, I would think we should be all right."

The news that Bertie would even consider selling his shop and leave his flat so surprised me that I had no response.

"No argument then," he continued, "we'll both stay here and see what we can turn up. Besides, where in all of England could one find so many exquisite birds? Vince, I do believe I see a Woodchat Shrike in that nearest tree. My word, it's just terrible that such a lovely place has been so despoiled."

We re-crossed the wooden bridge and headed back to the heart of the village, stopping here and there along the way to do a little birding. Shortly after noon, we made our way back to the *Forest City* pub. Eddie, having changed his clothes, was back behind the bar.

"Hope you enjoyed the sermon," said Eddie, looking Bertie in the eye. Then, with a disapproving look, he added, "Next time you'll have to stick around a little longer."

Bertie, without pausing to make any small talk or offer an apology, abruptly changed the subject. He asked Eddie flat out if he would be willing to rent us the room, for at least a week.

Bertie named what he thought was a fair price for both lodging and meals. Eddie agreed, albeit somewhat reluctantly, and we ordered drinks and Ploughman's lunches. After some encouragement from Bertie, I changed my lemonade order to a pint of the local brew.

The other patrons kept their distance as we ate, giving me the uncomfortable feeling of not being welcome. Even Bertie's winning ways seemed to have not made an impression on this lot.

Bertie, as usual, seemed not to notice. Instead he raved on about the beer. I had to agree. While I'm hardly a connoisseur, the beer at the *Forest City* pub was definitely tasty.

Ultimately, Sam, a stern looking, rotund fellow of indeterminate age, pulled up a chair and joined us. Sam wasn't much interested in small talk either, as he got to the point immediately.

"Do you gents really think it's wise to spend the week in Avalon?" Sam asked.

"How long have you lived here?" I replied, feeling a bit put off by Sam's question.

"Since before the war." said Sam. "But, as I believe Eddie told you, we didn't find out until some years ago that the army base, next door, had polluted this entire valley."

"It doesn't seem to have had much effect on you," I replied. "You look pretty healthy to me. So do the other people in the village."

"Aye, I'm healthy as an ox. But I was raised here. From what the scientists from the Ministry of Defence tell us, the pollution accumulated ever so gradually in our valley. Those of us that have spent most of our lives here have built up a resistance against the awful stuff. You blokes, however, aren't immune. Mates, if I were you I'd get in my fine little black motorcar and drive out of here, as fast as I could. Mind you, I don't want to sound inhospitable, but that would be in your best interests." With that Sam rose from his seat and left us to the remnants of our lunches.

Bertie looked worried. I was, however, even more determined to stay in Avalon – and to have Jenny's ashes buried in the churchyard.

"Bertie, as I said before, I'm staying here for a while. In my state of health, I'm not worried about pollution. But maybe you should consider leaving. I don't want you getting sick, or worse, on my account."

"No, I'll stay the week. Besides, I do want to meet Mr. Bobby Kipling, the alleged Canadian with the son who's such a Cleveland Indians' expert. We've come too far not to pursue that potential connection to the survivors of the *Susan Rae*."

"Yeah," I replied, "he does seem to be the only possible link left to our five American flyboys."

After finishing lunch we walked to the bar to pay our bill. I asked Eddie if I could meet with the village vicar. That request seemed to unsettle him even more than our decision to stay the week in Avalon.

"The vicar is in London, on business. He should be back late tonight. I should see him this evening. I'll tell him you'd like to talk with him," said Eddie. Admirably, he didn't inquire into my reasons for wanting to see the vicar.

"Eddie," said Bertie. "Do you often fill in for the vicar? I apologize for walking out on the sermon, but – from the bit I heard – it was jolly good. I particularly liked that part about there being no beer in Hell."

"Worse thing I could think of," replied Eddie, blushing. "As to filling in for the vicar, I do that on occasion. We're a small village and we all pitch in when the need arises. Besides, when you think about it there's not a lot of difference between being a bartender and being a vicar."

"How's that?" asked Bertie.

"Well," replied Eddie, "we both spend most of the day doing pretty much the same thing … listening to people's problems. The solution that the vicar always recommends is a prayer; the one the bartender recommends is another pint."

"Hadn't thought of it that way," said Bertie. "But I do believe you may be right."

I decided to change the subject. "Eddie, would you know just why they changed this village's name from Withington-in-the-Marsh to Avalon?"

Eddie shook his head, but an old man seated at the bar spoke up. "We can thank Doug Stevenson for that," he said.

Bertie took a seat at the bar and I followed suit. "Who," asked Bertie, "was this Mr. Stevenson?"

Eddie interjected. "This here's George Blackett. George was born in the village and probably knows more about the history of Avalon than anyone else in the village."

George gave us a smile and then answered Bertie's question. "Doug Stevenson, God rest his soul, was the village school's headmaster for more than fifty years. Lovely man; passed away just last year. He, and his best mate, Bobby Kipling, came here from Canada. If it weren't for them – particularly Doug Stevenson – there wouldn't be an Avalon."

"I'm not at all sure I follow you, George," I replied. Bertie nodded in agreement.

George pulled out his pipe, lit it, and leaned back in his chair. It was clearly story-telling time. I could only hope there would be some truth in what he had to say.

"This little village, as you said, used to be named Withington; Withington-in-the-Marsh to be precise. During the war the army moved everyone out. They said they needed the whole bloody valley, including the village. The villagers were told that the village would be destroyed, and that they would have to find other places to live. They said that we'd have to make a sacrifice, for the sake of the war effort."

George paused for a moment to blow a few smoke rings. He watched them slowly rise to the ceiling of the pub, and then continued. "We were given just three weeks to pack up and leave. My family relocated to Loughborough, in the Midlands. Other families wound up in other places. The villagers were spread about most of England. It was heartbreaking."

I stared at George in disbelief. "You're telling us that the army, your very own British Army, moved everyone out of this village. Why would they do that?"

"Vince, they did that during the war," said Bertie. "The military relocated people from a number of villages. They used the villages for training … you know, for practicing house-to-house combat. That sort of thing. Many are still deserted. In some cases it's simply too dangerous to return. In others there's simply nothing to return to."

George nodded in agreement. "That's a fact. Like I said, if it hadn't been for Doug Stevenson and Bobby Kipling, there would be no Avalon."

"What exactly did they do?" asked Bertie.

"They managed, somehow, to get the government to allow the villagers, at least those of us who were left, to return to the village. That was toward the end of the war. Doug Stevenson knew people in high places; he was a very convincing man. They listened to him. Bobby Kipling took care of the paper work and red tape. Between the two of them, they put this village back together. They're the reason that there's an Avalon."

"But," I replied, "how is it that two Canadians wielded that much influence on the British government?"

"No one knows for certain," said George, "and it didn't seem right to pry. We were just happy to have our village back. What most people believe is that the pair did something very important in the war. Our government must have felt they owed them. Doug and Bobby didn't like to talk about it; modesty, I suppose."

"You said something about the villagers 'who were left' returned to the village. What did you mean by that?" asked Bertie.

"Well, besides being evacuated from the village, our people ran into even more bad luck. Every village man who was able enlisted. All, sadly, in the same regiment. I tried to enlist but, because of my eyes, was rejected." George sighed and pointed at his glasses. They certainly had the thickest coke-bottle lenses I had ever seen.

"Lucky thing for me, I suppose. Most of that contingent was lost, in the North African campaign. That's where my two older brothers died. Toward the end of the war we were told that we could return to the village, but that it would remain within a military district, and under certain restrictions. We didn't give a fig about that; we just wanted to come home."

"Why the change in the village name?" asked Bertie.

"That was Doug Stevenson's idea. He thought that Withington wasn't a proper name for this village. For one thing, there's another place in England – in Gloucestershire – with the same name. But Doug thought there was an even more important reason to change the village name. Why, Doug asked the villagers, should such a lovely village be named after some indolent family whose sole contribution to England was that one of their ancestors stuck a knife in the back of one of the King's enemies? He recommended we name the village Avalon, like the city in the King Arthur's stories. We voted, and Avalon it became, and Avalon it is."

"Were there just two Canadians?" I asked. "You said that Doug Stevenson died recently. We know that Bobby Kipling is still alive, but were there any others?"

"Just the two," said George. "Only Bobby Kipling is left." George paused for a moment to blow another smoke ring and then added "And I'm afraid that he's not doing too well. Not likely to last out the summer, I hear. Tragic, that."

"This Bobby Kipling, would he happen to be a fan of the Cleveland Indians?" I asked.

George looked genuinely puzzled. "What's the Cleveland Indians?" he asked.

"Never mind," I replied. "What about his son, has he always lived in the village? Did he ever spend anytime overseas, in the States?"

We had clearly pressed George to his limit. Bertie gave me a warning look. George shook his head. "Walter's been to the States a few times, but he's spent most of his life in the village. Gents, why all these questions about the Kiplings?"

"Just curiosity, George," said Bertie. "Vince and I just find your lovely village very interesting. Nothing more than curiosity."

15
SUNDAY AFTERNOON, 27 APRIL 1997:
THE LOCAL BREW

After lunch at the *Forest City*, Bertie suggested we take a leisurely Sunday drive and do a little exploring. He also claimed that the Morris Minor needed the exercise.

Our drive through the narrow streets of the village confirmed our first impression. It was, in a word, lovely and, from all outward appearances, unspoiled.

The countryside was equally gorgeous. We agreed that this was certainly one of the most beautiful places in England. Whatever was polluting the area certainly had not harmed the scenery.

Hedgerows neatly separated the farm fields. This pleased Bertie to no end as, so he informed me, hedgerows provide nesting places for many of the local birds, as well as homes for other creatures such as hedgehogs. The land seemed particularly well cared for – not so much as a scrap of paper to clutter the landscape and absolutely no sign of graffiti anywhere.

Bertie pulled into a lay-by and parked the car. Shutting off the engine, he turned to me. "Vince, I'm having second thoughts about selling our story to *Hello! Magazine*."

"Why's that?" I asked, even though I felt I had a pretty good idea as to the answer.

"Even if we do locate the Yanks, I'm worried that any publicity about this matter would bring in swarms of tourists.

That would just ruin this place. Little Avalon and the surrounding countryside would soon be chock-a-block with tourists, their cars and caravans. Some eager entrepreneur is likely to open a Little Chef, or MacDonald's, or even a Tesco. Londoners will buy up the farmland and build swarms of their 'adorable' little two-million pound country cottages. Vince, in no time this place will be as awful as Stratford-on-Avon or, God help us, Windsor. I certainly don't want to be responsible for that."

"You're forgetting one thing, Bertie."

"What's that?"

"The pollution. Once people hear about the pollution, I'd doubt that there'd be many visitors," I replied. "That's hardly a tourist magnet."

"You're right, Vince. But what if we wrote about the pollution and how it's destroying the loveliest village in all of England? Perhaps there's some way to rid the area of the pollution, and our story could at least draw attention to the problem."

"That's not a bad idea, Bertie. If there's any hope left in saving the region, a story like that just might get people's attention. Maybe that would shame the government into cleaning up the mess their army left here – assuming that's possible. But that could just present another problem."

"Oh my, yet another problem," Bertie replied with a sigh.

"Right. If it is possible to clean up the pollution, then the village – or at least the attractiveness of the village – might still be lost. After all, once the pollution is removed, and after all the publicity, we're back to square one – a non-stop flow of tourists into the village. The fast food places. The hypermarkets. The souvenir stands. Streets jammed with cars. And all the fat tourist bottoms that this lovely little place will attract. I'm beginning to think that's the worst type of pollution."

"This is not an easy decision," replied Bertie, shaking his head. "Why don't we put it on hold until we solve the puzzle of the five Yanks?"

"I agree. What's your suggestion as to our next steps?" I asked.

"While you get things straightened out with the vicar, as to burying Jenny, I'll see what I can find out about Bobby Kipling. We know that his son seems to be an expert on the Cleveland Indians, and that Bobby's supposedly a Canadian. My bet is that Bobby Kipling is one of the five Yanks we've been looking for. Let's solve that mystery before we decide on anything else."

#####

Bertie turned the ignition key and the engine on the Morris Minor, faithful as ever, began its familiar hum. Bertie performed a somewhat shaky three-point turn and we headed back toward the village. After driving about a quarter mile he once again pulled the car to the side of the road and turned off the engine. This time, however, he rolled down the driver's side window and sniffed the air like some deranged red-haired bloodhound.

"Do you smell what I smell?" asked Bertie. "I thought I smelled something familiar the first time we passed this point. Now I'm certain."

"You're right. I definitely smell it. Smells like a brewery."

"That's my guess, Vince. Quite a pleasant smell, don't you think? Based on the way the wind's blowing, I'd say it's coming from that building to our right." Bertie pointed to what appeared to be an exceptionally large barn sitting about three hundred yards off the side of the road.

The "barn," or "brewery," was built of limestone, the same as virtually all the buildings in the countryside and village proper. It looked, however, much newer. Unlike the other buildings we had seen, there was no sagging roofline or any even slightly out of plumb walls.

"Looks new," I said. "Or at least new compared to everything else."

"Yes," Bertie agreed. "Probably not more than thirty or forty years old, at the most. Quite a large brewery for such a small village, don't you think?"

"I suppose so, but I have to admit I'm not much of an expert on breweries, or beer. Perhaps the villagers may just drink a lot of the stuff. If that's where they make the beer they've been serving us at the pub, I wouldn't blame them."

"Perhaps, but it still seems overly large," said Bertie, shaking his head.

"You don't think they're selling this stuff to pubs in other places, do you?" I replied. "Given the fact that this place is polluted, I'd think that would be illegal – or at least immoral."

"I don't know the answer to that, Vince, and I don't think it would be wise to pry – at least not yet. Whatever is going on, it's none of our business. Let's focus on Jenny's burial and the five Yanks."

"All right, but before we leave the subject of the brewery take a look at that cluster of trees, about fifty yards from the far end of the building. What do you make of that?"

"Let me get my birding binoculars," said Bertie, reaching into one of his book boxes on the rear seat. It seemed that Bertie had come prepared for any eventuality.

Bertie quickly found his binoculars, adjusted them, and scanned the area in question. He then handed the instrument to me.

"Have a peek, Vince. There are three lorries parked behind those trees. Each of them painted in regulation army camouflage. Behind them are four white vans."

"You're right," I replied. "I suppose the vans make sense, but why the military lorries? Good lord, you don't think that they're selling their beer to the Army, do you?"

"Don't know," answered Bertie. "Strange little village, this Avalon."

That evening we went downstairs for dinner. Eddie and Martha were behind the bar. Martha gave us her customary weak smile and took our order. Bertie ordered what was becoming his "usual," fish, chips, extra mushy peas and a pint.

"I'll have the same," I said. "By the way, is the beer local? I don't see any brand names on the taps."

Bertie gave me a particularly withering look. But it was nothing compared to the face Martha put on.

It was Eddie, however, who answered. "The beer is indeed local. Bobby Kipling has a small brewery outside the village. Quite good, don't you think?"

With that, Eddie walked over to us and, his face no more than a few inches from mine, continued. "It's probably not a good idea to drink too much of the local brew, or even the water for that matter. A little is not likely to harm you, but you never know. We do have bottled drinks from the outside. You might want to consider those."

"I'll stick with the local beer," said Bertie, "it's brilliant." I nodded in agreement.

We ate our dinner in silence. It wasn't until we finished that Bertie finally spoke.

"I thought we agreed that there'd be no questions about the beer."

"I know. I apologize. But you've got to admit that it's damn interesting that Eddie claims that there's just a small brewery outside the village when we both know that the place is quite large. And he admitted that it wasn't a good idea for outsiders to drink the beer."

"Yes,' said Bertie, "and then there's the matter of the three lorries in camouflage paint behind the brewery. But still, keep your mind on what we're here for."

16
MONDAY, 28 APRIL 1997:
THE VILLAGE VICAR; THE VILLAGE BUTCHER

On Monday morning it was the alarm on my travel clock, not the sunshine, that woke me up. The day was overcast and drizzly. A "fresh" day as the English – or my Jenny – would say. I felt surprisingly well and attributed it to the switch from painkillers to aspirins and Marmite. Diana knew her stuff.

Martha prepared us our full English breakfasts. Neither she nor Eddie, however, joined us.

As I was finishing my second helping of black pudding Eddie entered the room. He informed me that the vicar had indeed returned last night and had agreed to meet with me at nine … at the Kitcatt & Son butcher shop on the high street.

I had Eddie spell out the name as I thought I hadn't heard right. It was, indeed, Kitcatt. Bertie assured me that Kitcatt was a proper old English surname and had absolutely nothing to do with candy bars.

While the name was odd, a butcher shop seemed an even odder place for a meeting, but given all that was peculiar about Avalon, I didn't question the arrangements.

Shortly before nine I approached the butcher shop. A white-haired man in at least his late sixties, but with the arms of an Olympic shot-putter, was unloading sides of beef from the white van parked in front of the shop. When he saw me he stopped what he was doing, wiped his hands on his apron, and extended a now only slightly less bloody hand for me to shake.

"Good morning," said the man, "you must be Vince. Eddie told me you'd be coming. I'm Henry. Henry Kitcatt. I'd be the son in Kitcatt & Son," he added, pointing to the sign above the entrance of the shop. "Eddie said you'd like to speak to me."

"You're the vicar?" I asked, trying to not look too bewildered.

"Oh yes, on most Sundays and certain other occasions, I'm the vicar. More often, however, I'm the village butcher. Our little village is too small and too remote, I'm afraid, to have a full-time man of the cloth. But enough of that, you don't look like the type of man who has time for small talk. Eddie said you had a serious matter to discuss. Why don't we go into the shop? I've an office in back that will give us some privacy."

Once we got to the office, Henry took a seat behind a small table, while offering me the only other chair in the room. There was nothing in the office to indicate that Henry Kitcatt had any spiritual inclinations. The only pictures on the walls were of cattle, pigs, and sheep. Still, the man claimed to be the vicar and it was the vicar I needed to talk to.

"Henry, what I have to say is likely to sound rather strange to you," I said, breaking the silence. "But be assured that I am absolutely serious. Dead serious."

"Go on," said Henry, "and be assured that, in my position as vicar, I do hear some staggeringly strange tales."

"Well then, add this one to your list. My wife, Jenny, passed away about two years ago. She asked that I bury her in England." I unrolled the print and pointed to the church. "Her last request was that her ashes should be buried *here*."

Henry's eyes widened. "My goodness, that looks like our church. Or at least very much like ours."

"It does indeed. Bertie and I – Bertie is Jenny's cousin – have been driving all over the South of England, trying to find a church that looks like the one in the print. The church in this village is the closest fit."

"And you want to bury your wife's ashes here?" asked Henry. "Wouldn't it be better to bury her some place nearer to home? Home being, I take it, the States."

"I promised her that I would bury her in England. She was born and raised here."

"But wouldn't you prefer to have her buried near you?" Henry replied.

"Yes, I would, and that's the second favor I have to ask of you. When my time comes I want to be buried here too, alongside Jenny. All that I'm asking is that Jenny and I be buried in Avalon. I'll pay all the expenses, in advance. And there will be a significant donation to the church, and village. In fact, I'm prepared to write a check now in the amount of fifty-thousand pounds."

Henry was speechless for what seemed like a full minute or so. Ultimately he composed himself and replied. "If it were up to me, the answer would be yes, even without the generous donation. But this is a matter that I'll have to put before the village parish council. I can't make this decision on my own."

"When can the council decide on this?" I asked. "I'd really like an answer as soon as possible."

"I'll call a meeting of the council this week. Now that Doug Stevenson has passed on, there's only the five of us. That would be myself, Eddie of the *Forest City* pub, Sam Portman, and Bobby Kipling and his son, Walter. Bobby is the council chairman, so I'll call him and request the meeting. In fact, I'll do that right now."

"Bobby Kipling? We were told that he's quite ill. Will he be able to attend the meeting?"

"Oh yes, if necessary we'll hold the meeting at Bobby's place. The meeting will be held, that I can promise you. However, I have only one vote, and I can't promise you that the decision will be in your favor. It's rare that anyone but

villagers would be buried in our churchyard. Either Eddie or I
will let you know the outcome of the meeting."

"I understand, and I appreciate your help in all this."

#####

Leaving Vicar Kitcatt's butcher shop, I wandered about the
village for about an hour or so, trying not to get my hopes up
with regard to the council decision. The more I thought about
it, however, the more I became convinced that my request
would be granted. After all, fifty-thousand pounds should be a
significant inducement, no matter what the villagers thought
of having an "outsider" or two buried here.

On my stroll through Avalon I stopped in front of an
"electronics and appliances" shop. Something in the window
caught my eye. More properly, it was the absence of
something that intrigued me. The displays in the shop window
included cameras, computers, printers, phones, and radios.
There weren't, however, any television sets – which reminded
me that I had yet to see evidence of a single TV in the village.

I walked into the shop and waited my turn as the woman
before me purchased a toaster. When that transaction was
concluded I asked the man behind the counter, whom I
assumed was the storeowner, if he sold television sets. That
seemed to amuse him.

"No, we don't sell tellies. There's not much call for them
in Avalon," he replied.

"Oh, I take it that the villagers don't watch much
television?"

"None. There's no reception in the village, and we're a bit
off the beaten path for cable."

"But," I asked, "what about satellite TV? Certainly you can
receive those signals."

Taking on a tired look, the man replied. "There's no way to
receive *any* television signals. We are able to pick up radio
broadcasts once in a while, but," he said, pointing toward the

shop door, "the army base directly to our north has some big, buggery aerials that interfere with television reception. If you want to watch the telly, you'll need to drive to Waddington-on-Bodmin, about fifteen or so miles south of here. Same goes for using mobile phones."

I thanked the storeowner and walked across the street to the village square. Unlike the other villages Bertie and I had driven through, this square was quite large – possibly two hundred feet across, and came complete with benches, grass, and an amazing array of flowers. In the very middle was a large gazebo. As the morning drizzle had stopped, I decided to grab an empty bench and watch the passing crowd. This, I hoped, would kill time until lunch, at which time I was to meet Bertie at the *Forest City*.

As I sat on the bench the smell of honeysuckles and spring roses filled the air. Two elderly ladies, knitting what appeared to be sweaters, sat and chatted to one another across the pathway. Catching me staring, each gave me an endearing smile, and then returned to the business of the day. Their crisp accents, something I had always detested about the English – at least those other than my Jenny – somehow seemed sweet and even melodious. I wondered what it would be like to be born and raised in a village like this. Would I go mad with boredom? Or would I learn to live what seemed like a less tense, possibly more rewarding life?

Shortly before noon I returned to the *Forest City*. Eddie was behind the bar and Martha was bringing a meal to a customer. After waiting twenty minutes or so, with no sign of Bertie, I ordered lunch – including a pint of the local brew. I finished my lunch, along with a second pint, a little before one-thirty. Bertie, however, failed to make an appearance. I found this disconcerting. While Bertie might fib, gossip, and sometimes babble on about the most trivial things, he was always punctual. Or at least he always had been.

I asked Eddie and Martha if they had seen Bertie. Neither had, but Martha mentioned that he had gone out – bird watching – shortly after I had left to meet the vicar.

I waited in the pub until half past two. Bertie was still AWOL. Knowing how much Bertie loved his food, and his beer, I became more and more concerned. I again approached Eddie and asked him where else in town food was served. Eddie advised me that there were two other possibilities, both teashops. It seemed hard to conceive of Bertie in a teashop, but, after receiving directions, I decided to visit both establishments.

No one at either teashop had seen Bertie. Hearing that, I was almost ready to panic. I headed for the side street where Bertie had parked the Morris Minor. It was still there, and from the looks of things had not been moved since we had last driven it. I then took another walk around and through the village and returned to the *Forest City*. Bertie had still not shown up, and even Eddie seemed worried.

"I'll check around," said Eddie, "but I would guess that your friend's fine. Perhaps he just got carried away with his bird watching and lost track of the time."

I agreed that was indeed a possibility and advised Eddie that I would be in my room and to let me know if Bertie showed up. For the next several hours I waited in the room, reading one of the several books that Bertie had brought with him. This one was a novel, titled *Twelve O'Clock High*. Not surprisingly, it was about B17s and England. I recalled that there had been a movie by that name, but I hadn't realized, until then, that it was based on a book. I began reading it to simply pass the time, but after about a dozen or so pages I was hooked.

The turning of the bedroom's doorknob interrupted my reading. In walked Bertie, a particularly silly grin on his face. Looking at my watch I saw that it was nearly eight.

"And where the hell have you been?" I asked, feeling a bit too much like a concerned parent berating his misbehaving child.

"Oh, Vince, I've had the most amazing day. Alice is just brilliant. She knows more about birds than any person or any book I've ever run across. It's been just a super, splendid, brilliant day."

"Bertie, we agreed to meet for lunch. It's now dinnertime. And who the hell is 'Alice?'"

"Alice is just the most wonderful person I've ever met. Ever! Smart, pretty, and a fellow birder."

"How did you meet this goddess?" I replied.

"Vince, do restrain the sarcasm. Alice is a wonderful, kind person. You'll get to meet her tonight. I've invited her to join us for dinner." Looking at his watch, Bertie continued. "And we'd better get a move on. Dinner's in twenty minutes."

"Where's dinner?" I asked.

"Here, Vince; here at the *Forest City*. Tonight's special is an English style sausage plate. Alice says it's a once a week specialty of the *Forest City*, and that no one can do sausages like Martha."

The English style sausage plate was as good if not better than Alice had promised. There was even a special beer of the week, a local concoction called the "Mists of Avalon" that came with the meal.

Alice, as Bertie had promised, was indeed brilliant. Pretty, pleasantly plump, and with hair of a color strikingly close to that of Bertie, she was, in a word, delightful.

During dinner I learned that Alice had been widowed some ten years ago. Her husband had died, victim of a heart attack, at a relatively young age. Their only child, a daughter, was a medical doctor, and was serving her internship in the States.

Alice, herself, had been trained as a nurse – one of three who served the bulk of the medical needs of the villagers. Just a few months ago, however, she retired from those duties so as to devote more time to her bird watching.

I guessed Alice's age to be about fifty, and found her very pleasant company. Bertie, on the other hand, was absolutely smitten. A silly, lovesick grin never left his face, and he even let Alice do the talking. Alice, for her part, seemed equally taken by Bertie. This was a turn of events I had not foreseen.

A little after ten-thirty I excused myself and returned to the bedroom. Alice bid me a good night, but Bertie seemed utterly unaware of my departure.

17
TUESDAY, 29 APRIL 1997:
THE PARISH COUNCIL

On Tuesday morning Bertie literally leapt out of his bed at 7 a.m. He let me know that he would be skipping breakfast this morning, and that he had already informed Eddie and Martha that there would be only myself at the table.

"Where are you off to in such a rush?" I asked, even though I was certain it had something to do with Alice. There seemed no other possible reason for Bertie to miss his favorite meal of the day.

"Alice is taking me to a spot where she believes there just may be a pair of red kites."

"Red kites? Are you talking about those paper and stick things children fly?" I replied, wondering if the two of them had either lost their minds or reverted to their second childhoods.

"Vince, *please*. A red kite is a bird of prey. They were virtually wiped out in this country by the end of the 19th Century. Thanks to a breeding program, however, these birds are being reintroduced into the countryside. They're quite magnificent animals, Vince. Wingspans on the order of six feet wide. The only red kites I've ever seen have been in books. I can't wait to actually see one in the wild."

"Well, have a good time. And good luck with your birding – and your red-haired bird. Give my regards to Alice."

I ate my full English breakfast alone that morning. As I was finishing my third helping of black pudding, Eddie appeared in the doorway.

"The parish council will be meeting this evening, concerning your request. If the meeting finishes on time I'll either see you in the pub or come to your room and let you know the results of the vote. If we go late, however, we can talk tomorrow morning."

"All right. But, Eddie, is there anything that the council would like to question me about?"

"No, according to the vicar the request you're making is straightforward. Like I said, I'll let you know the results. Right now, though, I've got lots to do."

With that, he abruptly left the room. There had been no smile, no best wishes, and no indication of how Eddie might vote. Hopefully, he was just playing his cards close to the vest. Hopefully, Henry Kitcatt would present a favorable argument on my behalf. At any rate, there was nothing to do now but wait.

I decided to try to not think about the council, or the vote. Instead, I thought it might be nice to visit the village church again. So I spent the morning at the church, and then sitting by the brook that ran alongside it.

The brook was exceptionally clear and fast running, about thirty feet wide and no more than three or four feet deep. While sitting there I took note of the many frogs and turtles that seemed to have made it their home. And there were certainly plenty of fish, wild brown trout – or so they appeared to my untrained eye. How, I wondered, do they manage to live here? Why hasn't the pollution killed them? Why, in fact, do all the humans hereabouts look so healthy? These thoughts were interrupted by the appearance of a man on the opposite side of the brook.

It was Walter Kipling, and he was carrying a fly rod and fishing gear. Our eyes met and he gave me a sullen nod, and then walked farther down the side of the brook, ultimately disappearing from sight behind a grove of trees. I had the sick feeling that neither he nor his father would look kindly on having Jenny and me buried here – or even on the same planet.

Forgoing a lunch at the *Forest City*, I bought some bread and cheese in the village, found a shaded bench in the town square, and ate my lunch there. George Blackett, the alleged town historian, wandered by and, seeing me, asked if I wanted some company. I assured him that I would be delighted to have him join me and offered to share my bread and cheese.

"Oh no, mate, just had lunch. Three pints in fact. Just thought you looked a little lonely sitting there by yourself."

"Yeah, you've got that right. I suppose I am feeling a bit abandoned. My friend Bertie is off in the woods looking for birds and most of the villagers seem, shall we say, a bit reserved."

"It's a small village, and we don't see many visitors. We English tend to be like that, you know. We're not like you Americans. But don't take that to mean that you're not welcome. I, for one, am pleased that you and your friend are here ... for a while. And I, for one, hope that things go well for you at the council meeting tonight."

"You know about the meeting? Do you know what I've requested?"

George relit his pipe and blew a few smoke rings before answering. "The whole village knows about the meeting and your request. As I said, it's a small village – and you're big news. So, I might add, is the matter of Bertie and Alice."

"I take it the entire village knows that Bertie and Alice have been out birding?"

"Oh yes," answered George, "they do make a fine couple; don't you think?"

"I suppose so. I must admit that I've never seen Bertie so happy. Quite over the moon. But we'll be leaving within a few days and I'm not sure that this little romance will lead to anything. After all, it's not likely that Bertie would want to chance staying in a place that's so polluted and so terribly dangerous. And it's not likely that Alice would want to leave here for a man she's only known a few days."

"Perhaps," said George, "perhaps. But then who knows what the future holds?"

My sarcasm as to the matter of the pollution had either gone over George's head or he wasn't inclined to discuss it. I decided to give it another push.

"George, about the pollution. I'm certainly no expert on the subject but, from what I've seen there's no visible evidence of any pollution, or of any impact from pollution. In fact, this appears to be the healthiest place I've ever run across."

"Oh, make no mistake. The army polluted the area. The villagers and the flora and fauna here have adapted to it, but it's dangerous … absolutely deadly … to anyone else. Make no mistake about that."

I let it go. George seemed sincere. Either that or he was an excellent liar.

I had an early dinner at the *Forest City* that evening. Martha informed me that Eddie had left for the council meeting around seven, and that the meeting should be over no later than ten. She also remarked as to how she hadn't seen Bertie all day, her customary weak smile replaced by a wide grin.

Bertie showed up with Alice around nine that night. The glow on both of their faces lit up the room. I explained to Bertie that I wasn't sitting up and waiting for him to return. Instead, I was waiting for the results of the council meeting.

"Ah, so they're holding the meeting tonight," he replied. "Good thoughts. We must have good thoughts." With that he ordered another round of beers.

The three of us drank our beers, but there was a minimum of conversation. It was clear that even Alice was concerned about the vote. About ten-thirty Eddie appeared at the pub door. He scanned the room, located me, and shook his head. Nothing more need be said.

"Oh no!" said Alice, who had witnessed Eddie's signal. "It can't be. I just can't believe that the council would be so small and petty as to deny such a reasonable request."

Bertie, for his part, seemed stunned … and angry. "Bullocks!" he said. "How could that group of frigging wankers be such complete shitheads?"

I'm not quite sure about the translation into American, but it was clear that Bertie was sorely exercised. Alice, for her part, agreed wholeheartedly with Bertie's assessment.

It was about then that Walter Kipling walked into the pub. When he saw me he quickly averted his eyes and proceeded to the far end of the room.

Bertie had seen Walter's entrance and immediately rose from his chair and, before anything could be said to stop him, hurried across the room in the direction of Walter Kipling. Alice gave me a worried look. I shared her concern as, physically, Bertie was no match for the massive Walter. I could only hope that Cousin Bertie would survive the night.

For the next twenty minutes or so Bertie and Walter sat talking. Judging from the reddened faces of both men, it was not a pleasant conversation. I wondered if I should wander over, thought better of it, and drank a third pint.

Ultimately Bertie returned to our table, his face and manner grim.

"I have a meeting with Mr. Bobby Kipling tomorrow noon," he said. Looking at Alice, he added, "We'll need to postpone our walk tomorrow. I have some business to take care of."

Alice nodded. Neither she nor I asked him the nature of the business. It seemed clear that Bertie was in no mood to talk. Feeling inordinately tired, I excused myself.

"We'll see you in the morning, Vince," said an unsmiling Bertie. "Alice has invited the two of us for breakfast at her place. Go to bed now and get some rest."

18
WEDNESDAY, 30 APRIL 1997:
BREAKFAST WITH ALICE

Alice's cottage sat on the edge of the village. To the east lay a lush, green forest full of, according to Alice and Bertie, every type of bird imaginable. To the west lay the village proper. The cottage itself was immaculate, light and airy. However, the mood at the breakfast table was anything but light.

"Folks," I said, finishing my fourth helping of Alice's delicious black pudding, "there's nothing that can be done about the vote. The parish council voted, and I lost. It's as simple as that."

"Oh," replied Alice, "but you mustn't give up. What the council did was wrong. It should not stand."

"I haven't given up," I answered. "Alice, can I trust you with a secret?" Bertie, whose eyes had until then not left the untouched plate of food in front of him gave me a puzzled look.

"Certainly," said Alice. "Whatever you have to say will not leave this room. You have my promise."

"Before we arrived in Avalon, Bertie and I had agreed that we would find some lovely place in England, some place that would not be disturbed, and bury Jenny's ashes there. At that time we had no idea that the church in Avalon so resembled the church that Jenny's mother had painted. In short, this is the perfect place to bury Jenny. So that's just what I plan to do – with or without the parish council's approval, but first I'd like to ask a favor of you, Alice."

"Consider the favor granted," Alice replied. "I think I already know what you want me to do."

"What's that?" asked Bertie. "I haven't a clue as to what Vince is hinting at."

"I believe that Vince would like for me to help pick out a spot in our woodlands, where Jenny could be buried. Is that it, Vince?"

"Not exactly. I intend to bury Jenny's urn beneath the roots of one of the Yew trees in the village churchyard. In fact, I intend to do it tonight."

"In the churchyard?" said Bertie. "That's madness. Someone might see you. You can't do that. Alice's idea makes more sense. There are some lovely places in these woodlands, not more than a half mile from this very cottage. If you bury Jenny there we could come to Avalon to visit Alice, and we could also visit Jenny. No one would suspect anything that way."

"No," I replied. "Jenny wanted to be buried in a churchyard and that's where I intend to bury her. And, once again, I intend to do so tonight." Bertie shrugged his shoulders and sighed.

"If that's what you want," said Alice, "then I will do what I can to help you. I'll make sure that no one disturbs Jenny's resting place. In fact I'll recommend, to the vicar, that a bench be placed under the Yew tree, next to Jenny's grave. That way we can be assured that no one will disturb her."

"That's not a bad idea," I replied. "Then Bertie and I could work in a walk to the church during our visits. No one would think there was anything strange about us sitting on the bench."

Alice agreed. Bertie, for his part, said nothing more about Jenny's resting place. Most disturbing of all, he barely touched his food.

I wrote Alice a check for a thousand pounds. She agreed to cash it and then use the money to purchase a sturdy bench. She would donate it to the church, with instructions to have it placed under the proper Yew tree. I suggested that a nameplate be added to the bench, in memory of her late husband.

Alice agreed, saying that the plate on the bench would be a nice touch. Not only would it throw off any suspicion, it would be a fitting memorial to her husband. Bertie listened in silence, neither approving nor disapproving of the plan.

I decided to change the subject. "Bertie," I said, "you never did say how you arranged to have a meeting with Bobby Kipling."

"Ah, that wasn't easy. I finally convinced his big ox of a son that either he let me meet his father or I would have to spill the beans."

"Spill the beans?" asked Alice. "What on earth are you talking about, Bertie?"

Without a second's pause Bertie answered. "Alice, dear, *everyone* has something in their past that they don't want known. All I told Walter was that I would have to 'spill the beans.' That was all it took."

"Bertie," said Alice, "you are a most amazing man."

I wondered if it really could have been that simple, but decided not to press Bertie, particularly in front of Alice. Once the breakfast dishes had been taken care of, Alice offered to show me the local bird life, to be followed by a viewing of her slides. It was a frightening thought but there was no way I could refuse. Bertie excused himself, noting that he needed to go back to the *Forest City*, and then on to his appointment with Bobby Kipling.

I walked Bertie to the door while Alice tidied up her kitchen. "Bertie, just what do you intend to talk to Bobby Kipling about?"

"I intend to confront him. I'm quite sure he's one of the five Yanks we've been looking for. And I don't believe the man's sick, as everyone keeps insisting. If he can make it through a parish council meeting, he's certainly well enough to talk to me."

"I have to agree. And perhaps you could raise another subject."

"What would that be?" asked Bertie.

"Confront him on the matter of the so-called pollution around here. I'm convinced that's a lie. By the way, have you discussed that particular subject with Alice?"

"I have. She assures me that it is a fact. And, Vince, I don't believe she would say that if it weren't true."

"I don't think so either. But confront the Kiplings on that matter anyway, if you would."

#####

I've never been much of a nature lover, and the only walking I've done for the past thirty or so years was to and from my office and the university parking lot. However, the walk through the woods to the east of the village was quite nice and, surprisingly, not nearly as tiring as I had anticipated.

Alice seemed to know the name for every tree, flower, and bird, and I had to admit that there were plenty of birds. No wonder Bertie and she had hit it off so well. But that just made me wonder what would happen when Bertie left Avalon. The pair of lovebirds seemed a perfect match, and it made me sad to think of them apart.

Bertie had promised Alice that he would be back by two, or possibly three at the latest. At half past two Alice received a telephone call. Bertie, she informed me, had called to say that he would be late.

Alice and I spent the afternoon chatting. I did my best to engage her in small talk, just as Bertie had advised, and discovered that I was able to learn a great deal about her in a relatively short time. She had spent but five years of her life away from Avalon, attending the University of Nottingham where she had earned a degree in nursing. It was there that she had met her late husband, and persuaded him to move to Avalon.

Richard, Alice's husband, had received his degree in agriculture and was convinced of a need to return to organic farming. As a consequence of his evangelizing, and being able to convince both Doug Stevenson and Bobby Kipling, the farms surrounding Avalon were free of pesticides and herbicides. This, Alice proudly noted, is why everything, including the beer, has such a fresh and natural taste.

I agreed that the local food and drink were exceptional, but could not resist another inquiry into the alleged pollution. Alice explained that the pollution was all too real, and that it had been her husband who had made the first request to have the valley tested for contaminants. The scientists sent in from the Ministry of Defence had confirmed his suspicions. The irony of having a pesticide and herbicide free valley that had ultimately been polluted from outside had not been lost on Alice.

I had to agree with Bertie's assessment. Alice certainly appeared to be telling the truth, or at least what she believed was the truth with regard to the pollution. In fact, while admittedly having known Alice for but a short time, I became convinced that she was incapable of lying.

It wasn't until after seven that evening that Bertie finally returned. I heard the familiar sound of the Morris Minor's engine as he pulled to a stop in front of Alice's cottage.

Bertie's manner was quite different from the morning. He seemed relaxed, if not almost smug.

"So, Bertie," I asked, "how did it go?"

"Quite well, quite well. Fine chap, that Bobby Kipling. Top notch. But enough of that, I've got a surprise for the two of you. We'll be having dinner at the *King George*, in Waddington, this evening. The motorcar's right outside. I suggest we leave now if we want to get there in time."

I shook my head. "I can't come, Bertie. As I mentioned this morning, I've got work to do tonight. By the way, I'll be needing the shovel we left in the boot of the Morris Minor."

"No, Vince, you don't have anything to do tonight except celebrate. I wanted to save this for dinner but perhaps I should tell you now. The parish council will be meeting again, tomorrow night. They're going to revisit your request. This time, however, I'm convinced the vote will be in your favor. In fact I'll guarantee it."

"How in the world did you accomplish that?" asked Alice.

"The power of persuasion," said Bertie. "I simply persuaded Bobby Kipling that he should be in favor of Vince's request. He, in turn, convinced his son that this would be the right thing to do. From what I was told, the previous vote was three to two against the request. Two of those three who voted no were Bobby and his son. The other no vote was by Sam Portman, that rather unpleasant fellow who advised us to leave Avalon – for the sake of our health. I suspect that the new vote will be, at the very least, four to one in favor."

"Bertie," said Alice, "you are my hero. Isn't that wonderful news, Vince?"

I had to agree that it was. Bertie had come through for me … and Jenny. I just wondered what sort of blackmail it had taken to change the minds of the elusive Bobby Kipling and his surly son.

"Vince," said Bertie, "Bobby would like to meet you. You and he are to meet tomorrow morning at the school headmaster's cottage, at ten, sharp. Do you know where that is, Alice?"

"Oh yes, it's the sweet little cottage between the church and the schoolhouse, across the brook. Just take the path west, from the church. You can't miss it. But why would he want to meet Vince there? That cottage has been empty since Doug Stevenson passed away."

"Well, like you said, it's next to the church. I suppose Bobby wants to help Vince pick out a spot for Jenny to be buried. Either that," said Bertie with a wink, "or he wants to do away with Vince."

"Now, don't say that," said Alice, not recognizing Bertie's frail attempt at humor. "Bobby Kipling may be a hard man, but he's a good man. Don't you worry, Vince, there's undoubtedly a good reason for meeting there."

After dinner at the *King George* that evening we dropped Alice off at her cottage. Bertie walked her to the door. I turned my head and fixed my eyes on the bonnet of the car but couldn't resist one sidelong glance. I watched as they kissed goodnight, then fixed my eyes on the car's windscreen. For some reason the sight of those two kissing delighted me. After thirty-some years of hell, Bertie had found happiness. It couldn't happen, I thought, to a nicer guy.

We returned to the *Forest City*, and to our room. Bertie was whistling as we climbed the stairs. If I'm not mistaken, the tune was *Zip-a-dee-doo-dah*.

As soon as we entered the bedroom I turned to Bertie. "All right, Cousin, now let's hear the *real* story as to your visit with the Kiplings. I'm guessing that the 'persuasion' you used was to threaten to expose Bobby Kipling as being one of the survivors of the *Susan Rae*. Am I right?"

"No, Vince, you're wrong. The real story is that it was amazingly easy. When I arrived at Bobby's house, it was Bobby, himself, who met me at the door. He invited me into his office, in the rear of his house. All the while he had that same grim look on his face that we've seen on his son. I have to admit that it was a decidedly cool reception. The man was definitely not in the mood for small talk. Instead, he just asked me straight out about my remark, to his son, as to 'spilling the beans.' He asked me just what I meant by that."

"So far, Bertie, it doesn't sound 'amazingly easy.'"

"Oh, but it was — although I have to admit that, at first, I was a bit put off by Bobby's manner. So, when Bobby asked me about what I meant by 'spilling the beans,' I decided to start off slow and easy — and save the matter of the five Yanks for later. Rather than answer his question about 'spilling the beans' I unrolled the print of the church and placed it on his desk. I explained that Jenny's mother had painted the scene and told him about Jenny's last request. I pointed out that the church in Avalon was by far the closest match we had found to the one in the painting — and that all we really wanted was to satisfy Jenny's last wish."

"That's pretty much what I told the vicar," I said. "And that's what the vicar told the parish council. I don't suppose Bobby Kipling was moved by that story the second time around."

"At first," said Bertie, "Bobby just stared at the print. He finally agreed that the church in the painting looked remarkably like the one here in Avalon. Then he asked me a lot of questions, first about Jenny, then about her mother, and finally about you. After I answered those questions his demeanor changed considerably. That's when he said that the council would meet again, to take another vote on the matter. He assured me that the vote would be in your favor."

"That's it? That's all it took?" I replied.

"That was it, Vince. It was that easy. Like I said, it was amazingly easy."

"But what about the five survivors of the *Susan Rae*? And the claims of the valley being polluted? Did you discuss those matters with Bobby Kipling?"

"I did. But first he took me on a tour of his brewery. Remarkable place. By the way, I asked Bobby about the lorries in military camouflage parked behind the brewery. He explained that they had been left by the army when the base was vacated, some years ago. The villagers decided to take advantage of them so as to maintain their privacy."

"I'm not sure I follow you," I said.

"I didn't follow it at first either. It's a rather convoluted scheme to keep up the pretense that this area is still an active military base. They send the lorries out to pick up supplies for the village. The lorries then come back here and offload their goods to the white vans behind the brewery, and the white vans deliver to the village shops."

"Seems like an awful of a lot of work to go through just to keep tourists away," I replied. "But you were going to tell me about your discussions as to the five Americans. How did that go?"

"Bobby actually initiated that conversation. When we finished the tour of the brewery, Bobby poured me a pint, fresh from the vat. While I was enjoying the beer he up and asked me what the two of us had been doing at the site of the old barracks."

"Ah," I replied. "I wondered when that would come up. Bobby's son certainly spotted us returning to the Morris Minor that day. He must have told his father that we were snooping around. So, what did you tell Bobby?"

"I told him the truth. I explained that we were on the trail of the five survivors of the *Susan Rae*, and I told him that we were convinced that he was one of them."

"That must have surprised him," I said.

"Not at all, Bobby just grinned. He informed me that some Americans had been indeed been based at the barracks during the war, but that they were all long dead. According to Bobby, they left the area in the spring of 1944. The Americans joined up with a Canadian Infantry regiment and took part in the D-Day landing. That's where the Americans were killed. Vince, Bobby assured me that the Americans who were located at the military base are all dead. He, in fact, gave me his sworn word."

I had to interrupt. "Hold on a second, Bertie, just how could Bobby Kipling know all this – unless he was one of the survivors?"

"Both Bobby Kipling and Doug Stevenson were located in the same military installation – the one north of here – and at the same time that the Americans were housed there. In the spring of 1944 the Americans asked to be allowed to return to the front. They were assigned to Bobby and Doug's infantry unit – a Canadian regiment, and they were all involved in the D-Day landings, in June of 1944."

Bertie looked to me for a response. I had none. This was not at all what I had expected to hear.

Bertie continued. "Bobby and Doug survived the landing. Their American friends did not. Bobby and Doug were, in fact, eyewitnesses to their deaths."

I shook my head. "Okay, assuming that's all true, how do you explain the fact that Walter Kipling – the son of a *Canadian* – is such an expert on the Cleveland Indians, or at least Tris Speaker?"

"Bobby Kipling is from a town in the south of Ontario, Canada called St. Catharines - the very same town that Doug Stevenson came from. Are you familiar with that place?" asked Bertie.

"St. Catharines? It's right across the border from the States, not all that far from where I was born and raised."

"That's right," said Bertie, "and not all that far from Cleveland. And that explains the picture of Tris Speaker in the *Forest City*. Bobby Kipling may be a Canadian but he is quite the fan of the Cleveland Indians, and an even bigger fan of Tris Speaker. He put that photo of Speaker in the bar when he owned it, and it's stayed there ever since. Until you came along, no one had a clue as to who was in that old photo. It was his private little joke."

"Hmm," I responded. "It seems like Bobby Kipling has an answer for everything. I've got to say, Bertie, that it all fits together a little too smoothly. Do you actually believe the man?"

"Vince, he swore to me that the Americans we've been hunting for are dead – every last one of them. He swore it, and I believe him."

"All right, let's assume then that the five Americans are dead. But that still leaves the cock-and-bull story about the pollution. Did you ask him about that?"

"I did," said Bertie.

"And?"

Bertie looked away before answering. "Vince, I can't talk about that. I gave Bobby my word."

"Okay, that's a good enough answer for me. Just as I thought, there is no pollution."

"Vince, as I said, I gave Bobby my word. You can draw your own conclusion. Let's just not talk about the pollution … ever again."

"All right, no more discussion as to the pollution. But I still find Bobby Kipling's story about the five Americans hard to believe."

"Vince, we were looking for conspiracies and cover-ups when, all the time, what we were being told was the simple truth. Those are the plain and simple facts – no matter how much we might want the legend of the five Yanks and the American village to be true."

"So, the search for the five Yanks is over. Do you still intend to write your story for *Hello! Magazine*?" I asked.

"No, there's no good to come of that. It's best to leave this little valley alone and undisturbed."

"What about Alice?"

"Now that's a problem … but one that I think can be solved. Vince, I'm mad about Alice. She's the best thing that ever happened to me, and I think she feels the same. But she doesn't want to leave Avalon and I, of course, can't live here – not with the pollution. We've talked it over and decided that I'd move to Waddington. That's only about a half-hour drive from here. I think that will work."

"You're actually going to leave London? For a woman you've only known a few days? And do you really think that a city mouse like you can adapt to life in the country? You need to realize, Bertie, that there aren't any trains, or tubes, or fancy restaurants, or museums, or whatnot here. Hell, Bertie, there's not even any television reception. It's going to be quite a change."

"Vince, I'm looking forward to it."

19
THURSDAY, 1 MAY 1997:
THE TALL CANADIAN

On the morning of May 1st both Eddie and Martha seemed inordinately cheerful. They even joined us for breakfast. No word was mentioned as to the forthcoming re-vote, but I was quite sure that they both were confident of the results of tonight's parish council meeting.

Immediately after breakfast Bertie excused himself and left. He didn't have to tell me where he was going; the look on his face said it all. I chatted with Eddie for a while and then, at about a quarter of ten, headed for the village schoolmaster's cottage. The day was slightly overcast, but still quite agreeable.

I passed a number of villagers on the way, and either it was my imagination or frame of mind, but it seemed as though they were much more pleasant. Then again, perhaps they had just gotten used to seeing me.

As I crossed over the bridge and passed the church I saw the two buildings Alice had mentioned. The small cottage was evidently the schoolmaster's cottage, now deserted. Beyond the cottage was a much larger building, not quite a stately mansion but still very impressive. It would seem that the little village of Avalon had a rather grand schoolhouse.

As I approached the schoolmaster's cottage I could see that someone had parked a motorcycle to the side of the building. It was a Harley-Davidson; a late 80's Low Rider if I wasn't mistaken. It was then that the door of the cottage opened.

Out stepped a tall man, perhaps six-foot four or so. His long straight white hair was down to his shoulders. Judging from his leather jacket, trousers, and boots I had to assume that he owned the Harley.

"Vince Collesano, I presume?" he said.

"That's me. I'm here to meet Bobby Kipling."

"I'm Bobby," he replied, extending his hand.

"Really? I guess I expected a much older man. One whose frail health would hardly allow riding about on a motorcycle." Someday, I thought, I will have to do something about my sarcasm. Bobby Kipling, fortunately, chose to ignore the dig.

"Vince, I'm seventy-five years old. Sometimes I feel like it. Other times I don't. Thankfully, today's one of those other times. Would you like to come inside?" he continued, opening the door of the cottage.

The cottage was bigger than it appeared from the outside. It was also considerably tidier than I would have guessed, at least for a cottage that hadn't been lived in for a year.

"My son and I cleaned up the place last night. Everything works except for the fridge, but Walter will be bringing a new one around later today. How do you like it?"

"It's a fine cottage," I replied. "I assume that someone is moving in?"

"*You* are, although it's evident that Bertie failed to tell you."

"No, Bertie didn't mention a thing about moving into this cottage. I hate to sound ungrateful, but I'm really not sure what's going on."

"Vince, this cottage belongs to me. It's been empty since Doug Stevenson, the former village school headmaster, died. Doug left it to me in his will. I've kept it up, and frankly didn't care much for the thought of anyone living here – at least until now. I told Bertie that this would be just the place for you. It's not far from the church, and just a few minutes from the village center. You'll be able to visit your wife's grave anytime you wish."

"Mr. Kipling, Bobby, I really don't know what to say. This is unexpected."

"No need to say anything. I will be charging you rent. I expect to be paid promptly, the first of every month. One pound."

"Did I hear you right? One pound? Isn't that a bit below the going rate? I can assure you that I'm quite willing to pay more."

"All I want," replied Bobby, "is one pound a month – and that you keep the place up. I've been coming here once a week to take care of things. Now you can do that for me."

"Bobby, thank you. You have no idea what this means to me."

"Before you thank me, there is one other thing."

I prepared myself for the worst. "What would that be?"

"I understand that you are a Cleveland Indians' fan. If you wouldn't mind, I'd like to meet with you, say once a month, at the *Forest City*. Drinks are on me. All I want is to chat about the Indians. Not much interest in baseball in these parts, and I'd really like to have someone else's opinion of the Indians' chances this year."

"You have a deal," I replied.

"Fine. It's been a pleasure meeting you, Vince. We can talk more, later. Right now I've got to get back to the brewery. There seems to be a problem with a sticky valve on a fermentation tank, and there's no way I can trust Walter to fix that. The boy is hopeless around anything mechanical. May I give you a ride back to the *Forest City*?"

"Thanks for the offer, but I'd like to take a stroll over to the church. And thanks again for the use of the cottage. You can be sure I'll keep things tidy."

Bobby Kipling shook my hand, placed a shiny black motorcycle helmet on his head and mounted the Harley. He turned and gave me one last wave as he crossed the bridge and headed back toward the village.

As Bobby Kipling disappeared from view I did my best to sort out my thoughts. It was my guess that Bertie had told Bobby that I had only weeks to live. That seemed the only thing that could explain the anticipated turn-around on the vote – as well as the one-pound a month rent on the cottage.

For a moment I felt angry, with much of my resentment directed toward Bertie. It seemed clear that the Kiplings had not changed their mind because of any logical argument that Bertie had presented. Instead, they were doing this out of pity. As I walked to the church my anger dissipated. What difference did it really make? The objective was to satisfy Jenny's final plea. That had been accomplished. There was no point in being angry with Bertie, the Kiplings, or anyone else. The mission I had set out on was almost finished. All that remained was to wait for the inevitable, and to then rest next to Jenny for eternity.

#####

That evening Eddie entered the pub at about half-past seven. He headed for our table with a smile on his face.

"Chaps, the vote was unanimous. The vicar suggested that the funeral be held Saturday morning. Vince, he wants to know if you'd like to have formal services prior to the burial of the ashes."

"That's wonderful, and I'm really grateful for the vote of confidence. But, as to a funeral and services, that's not something I had considered. What do you think, Bertie?"

"I think that Jenny deserves a proper burial. I think you should accept the vicar's gracious offer. But that's your decision," said Bertie.

I turned to Eddie. "Eddie, tell the vicar that I appreciate and accept his offer. I've got to say that this is the best news I've had in a long time."

"Fine, I'll let him know. And, if you don't mind, Martha and I would like to attend the services."

"I'd love to have you and Martha attend. I only wish you could have met Jenny. She was, as Bertie can confirm, a very special person."

"The best," said Bertie.

"There's one other thing," said Eddie. "Bobby Kipling would also like to attend. Would that be all right with you?"

"Of course," I replied, not knowing what else to say.

20
SATURDAY, 4 MAY 1997:
A STRANGER AT THE DOOR

Bertie and I moved our luggage and boxes to the cottage on Friday. He let me know that he and Alice would be leaving for London immediately after Jenny's burial. He planned to sell his news agency shop to Nigel, close up his flat, and then find a place to live in Waddington. Bertie estimated that he and Alice would be away for two to three weeks.

His only concern was for me. He was extremely uneasy about leaving me on my own.

"Vince, come with us. While I'm taking care of business you and Alice can take in the sights. Once I clear everything up, we'll come back to Avalon. To tell you the truth, I'm not comfortable leaving you here by yourself."

I assured Bertie that I would be fine. In fact, I let him know that I felt better than I had in the past two years. Sometimes, in fact, I could almost forget that I was sick.

Bertie reluctantly agreed. He did insist, however, that he call every night to check on me. He also mentioned something about having Eddie and Martha look in on me. It was all a bit disconcerting … and comforting.

The funeral services on Saturday morning were lovely. As promised, Eddie and Martha were in attendance, along with Bertie, Alice, and the vicar. Bobby Kipling was also there, although he kept to himself and seemed, to me, distinctly uncomfortable. The weather was perfect. The sun was shining, the sky was blue, and the birds were singing their feathered little heads off - enough so that Bertie and Alice were able to determine that at least two dozen distinct species were in the trees surrounding the church.

Bertie gave the eulogy. He put into words the admiration and feelings I have always had for my wife, and for that I will always be thankful. I realized that just having Bertie around lessened the pain of losing Jenny. My dear Jenny, I realized, was a much better judge of people than me. She had seen the goodness in Bertie, while I had fixated on his faults.

When Bertie finished, Henry Kitcatt, full-time butcher and part-time vicar, read the *23rd Psalm*, Jenny's favorite passage from the Bible.

> *The Lord is my shepherd; I shall not want. He maketh me to lie down in green pasture; he leadeth me beside the still water. He restoreth my soul; he leadeth me in the paths of righteousness for his name's sake. Yea though I walk through the valley of the shadow of death, I will fear no evil; for thou art with me; thy rod and thy staff they comfort me. Thou preparest a table before me in the presence of mine enemies; thou anointest my head with oil; my cup runneth over; surely goodness and mercy shall follow me all the days of my life; and I will dwell in the house of the Lord forever.*

Although I have heard that prayer many times before, this was the first time I had really understood the meaning of the words. Perhaps it was just the fact that it was the first time I had truly listened. I really felt that I could walk through the valley of death without the fear and dread that had so permeated the past two years of my life. It was, in fact, the first time in two years that I really felt at peace.

Once the reading concluded Martha sang Jenny's favorite hymn, *Just a Closer Walk with Thee*. Martha's voice was as clear and light as the soft English morning, and I had to struggle to keep my composure. It was a lovely funeral, in a lovely place, and I was sure that Jenny must be pleased.

#####

After the services Bertie and Alice departed for London in Alice's car, a cherry red 1993 Morgan Plus 8. The top was down and the pair of lovebirds waved goodbye as they sped off into the distance. All in all it had been, I decided, a very good day.

Before leaving, Bertie had told me that he no longer had any need for anything in the "book" boxes we had been toting all over England. He said I could do whatever I wished with the contents. That evening I decided to unpack the boxes and throw away anything not of interest. It was, I discovered, an eclectic collection.

In addition to old and new ordnance survey maps, Bertie had packed file folders full of information about the *Susan Rae* and its crew. There were even two enlarged black and white photographs. One showed the crew members standing beside the aircraft. The other was of a group of young airmen, whom I assumed were the same crew, seated at a table in a pub. The date scrawled on that picture was 16 December 1943. That would make it less than a week before the *Susan Rae* crashed into the pasture behind the house of a young Tom Hawkes.

I took yet another, closer, look at the picture of the crew in front of the plane. In that photograph the aircraft's name, the *Susan Rae*, was painted on the nose. Under it was a drawing of a buxom blonde wearing a 1940's style bathing suit, in a classic Betty Grable pose. There was something about the photograph that bothered me.

I searched among the box contents until I found the photograph that Tom Hawkes had given to Bertie in the *Errant Hun* during our stopover in Lower Friththingden. There was one obvious and striking difference between the aircraft in the pasture behind Tom Hawkes's house and that earlier one with the crew. There was no nose art on the downed plane. There was, in fact, no name whatsoever on the nose of the aircraft lying in the pasture. Yet this was the picture that Tom Hawkes had taken immediately after the plane had crash-landed, and well before anyone on the ground could have had a chance to paint over the nose of the aircraft.

I decided to keep all the material, and to read the documents thoroughly over the next few weeks – or whatever time I had left. I placed the photograph of the *Susan Rae* and that of the plane that had crash-landed on the kitchen table. I imagined that Bertie might find them interesting. Then again, he seemed to have lost all interest in the *Susan Rae* and its crew.

About seven that evening I thought I heard a timid knock on the cottage door. For a moment I wasn't sure if I hadn't imagined the noise. However two slightly more distinct taps followed.

I opened the door to find Walter Kipling looming before me, carrying a large cardboard box. The six and a half-foot, twenty-two stone behemoth greeted me with his customary glare. For a moment I thought about slamming the door shut and locking it. Then again, it was apparent that Walter, England's answer to the Incredible Hulk, would hardly be stopped by something as insignificant as a solid oak cottage door. Walter, his face slowly turning red, finally broke the silence.

"Good evening, Professor Collesano," he said, in a soft voice. "I came to see if the new fridge was working properly. I've also brought some of my meat pies and black pudding. Eddie tells me you're quite fond of black pudding, and I'm told that I make the best black pudding in the South of England."

Feeling quite the fool, I simply stood there staring at the man.

Walter Kipling, his face now the color of a ripe tomato, continued his monologue. "If you like fish, I'll bring some fresh caught trout by whenever you would like. You do like fish, don't you?"

"I do," I replied, finding my voice. "I like fish very much, and I'm absolutely wild about black pudding. And, by the way, the new fridge seems to work perfectly."

"That's good to hear," said Walter, still standing in the doorway. "Would you like for me to help you put these in the fridge?"

"Oh, yes, that would be great. Excuse my manners; do come in. And please call me Vince. I assume it is all right to call you Walter?" In reply Walter simply nodded his head.

Walter followed me into the kitchen and placed the cardboard box on the kitchen table. There must have been two-dozen packages in the box, each carefully wrapped in aluminum foil. I opened the refrigerator door and Walter handed me the packages, one-by-one. He wasn't, however, looking at me. Instead he was staring intently at the two photographs that I had left on the table.

It was an odd and uncomfortable moment. However, Walter asked no questions about the photos. Instead he spent the next few minutes advising me as to how to warm up the pies and black pudding.

Walter was a man of few words. Despite his appearance and gruff manner he seemed a gentle soul. He was also well spoken, and apparently well educated. Walter Kipling was a human personification of the saying; "you can't judge a book by its cover."

Once Walter was convinced that I understood the directions as to preparing the pies and pudding, he excused himself and headed for the door. As his large hand encompassed the doorknob I decided to ask him another favor.

"Walter, I saw you fishing the other day. Fly-fishing from the look of it. Would you be interested in some company on your next foray?"

The big man turned, smiled, and replied. "I'd very much like your company. But I tend to go fishing almost every day so just let me know when you'd like to try your hand at catching our local trout."

"How about Monday?" I replied.

"That won't be possible," said Walter. "I'll be leaving for Scotland tomorrow evening, and I won't be back until the fifth of June. How about June 6?"

We agreed to meet the morning of June 6th, outside the village church and next to the bridge. I could only wonder if I would still be above ground on that date.

Walter reached out and shook my hand. It was like being gripped by a vise. This giant of a man might be soft-spoken, but he was clearly as strong as he looked.

When Walter left I proceeded to heat up one of his pies, a steak and kidney. It was fabulous. While I sat there enjoying the pie I did wonder how the man could possibly spend almost *every* day fishing. Did Walter Kipling not have a job? And what about the photographs? Had he recognized the aircraft? I supposed that I would ultimately find out the answer to the first question. However, it seemed that the second would likely remain a mystery.

Finished eating, I cleaned up the kitchen. It was then that I decided to put the two photographs away. Bertie had moved on; the *Susan Rae*, its crew, and the American village no longer held his interest.

21
5 MAY THROUGH 5 JUNE 1997:
AN ODD LITTLE VILLAGE

A few days following Jenny's funeral Bertie telephoned to let me know that his business in London was going to take longer than he had anticipated. Not only did he have to transfer his news agency to Nigel, he would also have to provide Nigel with some rather extensive training. It seemed that Nigel, although an excellent mechanic and eager to learn the news agency business, was hopeless when it came to bookkeeping.

Bertie had also decided to sell the building that housed the news agency and his flat, as well as two nearby buildings that he owned. That particular bit of news was a stunner. I had not, until then, realized the extent of Bertie's real estate holdings.

I let Bertie know that I was fine and that Eddie and Martha were looking in on me. I was eating a full and hearty English breakfast every morning, and getting my required two tablespoons of Marmite each day. The truth was that I was feeling surprisingly well and had been taking regular walks every morning.

Bertie assured me that he and Alice would be back in Avalon by no later than the second week in June. He also mentioned that they had a surprise for me.

I spent the month of May taking leisurely morning walks; ultimately working up to five mile hikes. I intended to be in as good a shape as possible for my June 6th fishing trip with

Walter. And I was becoming more confident that I might actually be around to make that date.

Most days I ate breakfast and lunch in my cottage, and then spent the afternoons working in the garden. Lily, the church organist, would often drop by and supervise my efforts. She had, I later discovered, a degree from Oxford in horticulture, and the gentle lady definitely knew her stuff.

In fact, it seemed that a surprising number of the villagers had attended university, and several had graduated from some of the most prestigious schools in England and America. Yet, from all outward appearances, they seemed ordinary, hard-working country folk. Appearances, particularly in the odd little village of Avalon, could be deceiving.

Each weekday morning a parade of children passed my cottage on the way to school. Each afternoon they took the same path home. Dressed in crisp, attractive school uniforms, they were unfailingly polite, and I soon got to know each of them by name. They seemed particularly intrigued by the fact that I was an American. I found myself intrigued by the fact that they literally besieged me with questions about that lost colony across the big pond. I soon found, however, that they seemed to know more about the history and geography of the United States than had my students at university. Education, in Avalon, was evidently taken very seriously.

My trips into the village for food and supplies were also an education. Henry Kitcatt did not just sell meat; he provided menus and advice on how to cook his wares. The same was true for the village baker and the owner of the village grocery. Arnold Davis, the village ironmonger, provided me with advice on the selection and proper use of gardening tools, as well as on the choice of seeds. Of course it helped that Arnold was the husband of Lily, the lady with a graduate degree in horticulture.

I also discovered that Martha, Eddie's wife, was the village treasurer and served as financial advisor to virtually all the villagers. Martha was, according to the regulars at the *Forest*

City, the reason why nearly every family in the village had at least one fine car.

Those automobiles, however, were rarely seen unless their owner was off on a trip to some other village or town. The streets of Avalon, in fact, were virtually devoid of anything with an internal combustion engine, other than the occasional sighting of Bobby Kipling's motorcycle or an unmarked white van making a delivery to one of the village shops. In Avalon, the mode of transportation for any trip under five miles was apparently either one's feet or a bicycle.

Several evenings a week I took supper at the *Forest City*. Each night there was a different special, all quite good and each prepared under Martha's close supervision and according to her own recipe. My favorite, however, soon became the Jugged Hare, followed by a dessert consisting of a selection of English cheeses. I did find that no matter what was served, or how delicious it might be, the local beer was the highlight of any meal.

By the end of May, and with considerable help and advice from both Martha and Henry Kitcatt, I was able to prepare a full English breakfast that came as close to matching Martha's as any mortal could hope to expect. For a man who had never prepared anything more complex than a bowl of cold cereal, I became quite proud of my culinary skills. So much so that I volunteered to prepare three dozen Shepherd's Pies, every Monday, for the school lunch. Based on the compliments I received from the children every Monday afternoon, the pies were well received.

Toward the end of May I had my second encounter with Bobby Kipling. It was Jugged Hare night and I was settling in for a feast. About a quarter after eight Bobby Kipling entered the *Forest City*. He walked to my table and asked if he might join me. In his left hand he was holding a copy of last Sunday's sports section of the *Cleveland Plain Dealer*.

So there I sat, across the table from a man with the Sunday sports section of the *Cleveland Plain Dealer* – a tall man with long white hair that rather conveniently covered his ears. I had the urge to confront him, but restrained myself. I was a guest in the village and, in fact, a guest in his cottage. If Bobby wanted to insist that he was not one of five Yanks we had been looking for, and if Bertie wanted to believe him, then I suppose it would be best for all concerned to let the matter rest.

So it was that the two of us spent the evening discussing the Cleveland Indians. It was Bobby's opinion that 1997 would be a great year. The Indians had won an even hundred games in 1995 and ninety-nine in 1996. In '95 the team had reached their first World Series since 1954.

The hitting and pitching, according to Bobby, looked solid. He was convinced that this just might be the year the Indians would win the World Series. I hoped he was right.

#####

On June 5th I received a call from Walter, who had returned from his somewhat mysterious trip to Scotland. He reminded me of our fishing trip that Friday, and that we had agreed to meet at the village church.

22
FRIDAY MORNING, 6 JUNE 1997:
D-DAY CELEBRATIONS

Bright and early on the morning of June 6th I met Walter Kipling at the church for our fishing excursion, just as we had agreed to a month earlier. He brought along an extra set of fishing gear for me, including what appeared to be a brand new rod and reel. The rod was of the finest bamboo, perfectly balanced, and the workmanship was remarkable. The gear was mine, he told me, to keep as long as I lived in the cottage.

"We've got till about eleven o'clock, and then it's on to the ceremonies. So we'd best be on our way," said Walter.

"What ceremonies?" I asked.

"It's June 6th," he replied, looking at me in amazement. "This is the fifty-third anniversary of D-Day. Surely you haven't forgotten?"

I had to admit that I had. I didn't mention the fact that I suppose I almost always had.

"One of my favorite spots is about three miles from here," said Walter. "Are you up to a walk in the woods?"

"As long as we're not climbing any hills I think I can handle it," I replied.

We followed the bank of the stream until we reached a spot that Walter proclaimed to be one of the best sites for trout in all of England. It certainly was tranquil. The stream itself had narrowed to perhaps twenty feet across and was considerably rockier than back at the church. In fact, lurking behind at least three of the rocks I could see the faint outline of trout. The most distant fish appeared to be a good eighteen inches in length.

There was a minimum of conversation that morning. It seemed that neither Walter nor I had much expertise in small talk. I did manage to catch and release five trout, most less than ten inches long. Walter, with his advantage of almost daily practice for nearly four decades, landed an even two-dozen – keeping three of the largest.

"These are for you," he said, handing me the string of fish as we prepared to leave.

On the walk back Walter was slightly more talkative. As we neared the church he asked if I would want to join him again on another fishing trip, this time to a lake located between Avalon and Waddington.

I agreed and we made plans for an early morning start on Monday. Walter would come by and pick me up at 5 a.m. It was then that I decided to pop the question that had been running through my mind for weeks.

"Walter, if this is not too personal, I've been wondering what sort of work you do. I've concluded that you're either independently wealthy or a professional fisherman. Which would it be?"

Walter grinned. "If you can keep a secret, I'll show you what I do for a living on Monday."

"I promise not to tell a soul," I replied, wondering if his occupation just might have something to do with serial murders. Then again, it seemed unlikely that this gentle giant would be involved in anything quite that nefarious.

"Ceremonies start at noon," said Walter, as he walked away. "I expect to see you there."

"Where would 'there' be?" I asked.

"The village square, of course. The event normally lasts an hour or so. After that almost everyone heads to the *Forest City*."

"I'll be there. By the way, I want to thank you for inviting me to go fishing this morning. It's been years since I last cast a line, and I've got to say I really enjoyed it."

Walter gave me a shy smile. "You're more than welcome. I enjoyed the company."

Shortly before noon I walked into the village and toward the village square. It appeared that every man, woman, and child in Avalon was there. It was clear that, in Avalon at least, D-Day was a very important day.

As I approached the village green I noticed that people were being handed folded sheets of yellow paper. However, as I reached out for one of the handouts I was ignored; rather deliberately ignored it seemed to me.

"May I have one of the handouts?" I asked, trying not to appear annoyed.

"Oh no, this would be of no use to a Yank," said the woman before turning her back on me.

I didn't know whether to feel hurt or angry. I decided to approach another leaflet bearer and see if I might not receive better treatment, and I have to admit that I was becoming curious as to just what was written on those flyers that seemed to be in everyone's hands but mine.

Astonishingly, I was met with the same response. The leaflets, I was told, were for British citizens only. Instead of the leaflet, I was handed a small flag. On one side was the Union Jack, on the other the Stars and Stripes.

I accepted the flag and joined the throng gathered round the gazebo. A few minutes later a hush came over the crowd as several dozen men, ranging in age from about the mid-twenties on up, marched solemnly up the path leading to the gazebo. They were all in uniform, although it was quite clear that some of them had outgrown their military costumes many years before.

I recognized several of the contingent. Bobby Kipling was there, leading the procession. He was wearing a Canadian Army Corporal's uniform. That would certainly fit with the story he gave Bertie, but I still couldn't help but wonder what the old man might look like in the uniform of an American Army Air Force airman.

Vicar Henry Kitcatt walked behind Bobby Kipling. From what I could tell his uniform was that of a private in the British Army. Eddie was there, in the uniform of a British Navy officer. Not to be missed was Walter Kipling, standing a head or so taller than most of the others. Walter was dressed in the uniform of an RAF officer, and it fit perfectly.

Following the men were a dozen or more women, some dressed in military uniform, others decked out in nurses garb. I overheard a woman next to me explain to her young son that the procession was restricted to those who had not just served in the military, but that they also must have seen actual combat in any British engagement since and including the Second World War,

As the group took their places on the gazebo, a cheer went up from the crowd. Henry Kitcatt walked to the microphone, and the ceremonies got under way.

The ceremonies started with a prayer, followed by several rousing speeches and appeared to conclude with yet another prayer. Rather obviously, the citizens of the tiny village of Avalon took the anniversary of D-Day very seriously. But the event wasn't, to my surprise, over yet.

Walter Kipling rose and was handed the microphone. A hush fell over the crowd and I expected a final speech. Instead Walter began singing. The song was "God Save the Queen." Walter, I concluded, was an extraordinarily fine tenor.

After the first chorus, the crowd joined in. It was, I thought, a very inspiring performance.

When the song concluded the crowd grew quiet again. Walter took his seat. His father stood and walked to the microphone.

"We have a guest today. Vince, would you care to join us in song?" said Bobby. "I'm quite sure you know the words," he added, looking directly at me.

I didn't know what to say. Luckily, I didn't have to say anything. Bobby began singing, softly at first and then stronger and louder. He may not have had the musical talent of his son, but he made up for it in volume.

The song was "God Bless America." At the conclusion of the first chorus the crowd joined in, reading the words from the yellow leaflets that I had been denied. This, I realized, had all been programmed. It had been done for me. It was a most excellent surprise.

23
MONDAY, 9 JUNE 1997:
CATHERINE CLOVELLY, ROMANCE NOVELIST
EXTRAORDINAIRE

I heard the sound of Walter's Land Rover a few minutes after five. I placed my fishing gear in the rear of the car and joined Walter in the front seat.

"Morning, Vince, ready for some truly fine fishing?"

"Oh yes, I've been looking forward to it." I decided that I wouldn't mention the fact that I was also looking forward to finding out just what Walter did for a living.

We arrived at the lake at around 6 a.m. There were a number of boats, each equipped with electric trolling motors, tied to a dock leading onto the lake. Walter's craft, a shallow draft wooden bass boat, was at the far end of the pier. We packed the boat with our equipment, food and drink, and headed toward the far side of the lake.

By 10 a.m. we had caught our limit. Bobby docked the boat on a small island in the center of the lake. We unloaded the food and what was left of the drinks and found a shady spot.

"Oops," said Walter, "I've forgotten something." With that he walked back to the boat and retrieved a small cloth bag. He sat down beside me, opened the bag, and handed me its contents. It was a paperback book, from the looks of the cover, a romance novel.

"You asked me what I do for a living. This is it," he said, pointing to the book. "And do remember you promised to keep this confidential."

I was mystified. I carefully examined the cover of the book. It pictured a dark-haired woman in the arms of a muscular, blond-haired Adonis. Behind them was a fairy tale castle, seated on the top of a hill. The title of the book was *Magic Knights*. The author's name, written in even larger letters than the title, was Catherine Clovelly. I looked to Walter for help.

"Turn it over," he said.

I turned the book over. On the back was a color photograph of a quite elegant looking middle-aged woman with long blonde hair. She was wearing a low cut gown that exposed some particularly scenic cleavage. The woman was standing next to a forest green Land Rover. Behind her was what appeared to be a stately home.

"Don't you recognize that scene?" said Walter, pointing to the picture.

"It looks like the village schoolhouse, and that looks like your automobile. But please, Walter, don't tell me that the woman is you in drag."

Walter chuckled. "No, a big hairy bloke like me would hardly make that dainty a woman. Take a closer look, Vince. Certainly you know who she is."

I looked at the picture again. I hadn't a clue. "I give up, Walter. I don't think I've ever seen this woman before."

Walter seemed disappointed. "Vince, that's Martha, Eddie's wife. She's wearing a blonde wig and some makeup, but that's most certainly Martha. I should know; I took the picture just ten months ago."

"Ah, so you're a photographer. Now I understand," I said, feeling like quite the dunce not to have figured it out earlier.

"No, Vince, you clearly don't understand. I write books. This is my most recent release. That's why I was in Scotland the past several weeks, to research my next book. I'm thinking of titling it *The Tattered Tartan*. It takes place in the highlands, during the time of the clearances."

"You mean to tell me that you write *romance novels*, under the name of Catherine Clovelly?"

"That's right. So far I've had forty-two novels published, *all* under the name of Catherine Clovelly. Do you really think that a romance novel under the name of Walter Kipling would sell? Now do you see why I asked you to keep this confidential?"

"I do, but you've got Martha's picture on the back of the book. Does she know?"

"Martha knows, and has been sworn to secrecy. Her picture has always appeared on the Catherine Clovelly's series. The only others that know are you, my mum, and my dad. Mum's proud but Dad will carry this secret to the grave. Of that you can be sure."

"And there's money in this?" I said. "Do you sell a lot of these?"

"Vince, you've obviously not been to a bookstore in the last twenty years, or at least to the romance novel section. Catherine Clovelly is considered to be one of the top romance writers in all of England. *Magic Knights* reached number three on the list of romance novel sales, and it's still in the top ten. There's definitely money in this."

"But why *romance* novels? Why not thrillers, or mysteries, or detective novels?" I stopped myself before asking: Why not something more manly?

"I don't know for sure. I just happened to pick up a romance novel while I was serving in the RAF. I was bored and depressed, so I read it. It was wonderful, one of the best that Barbara Cartland ever penned. The next week I began to write my first Catherine Clovelly novel, and I haven't stopped since."

"Wow, and you've written forty-two of these."

"Yes, forty-two in a little less than twenty years. I spend about four hours a day writing, and the rest of the day thinking about what I'm going to write next. A lot of people are under the impression that writing a romance novel is easy, that anyone can do it. I'm here to tell you that it's hard work, and it's lonesome work."

"Well, after forty-two successful novels, I'd think you could take a break – or retire," I replied.

"I didn't say I didn't like writing, I just said it's a hard and lonely profession. But Vince, there's nothing more satisfying than finishing a manuscript. The next best thing is seeing some woman reading your very own book on the seat across from you on the train. I can't even begin to explain the feeling that gives me. If I didn't have my writing I'm quite sure I'd be the village drunk."

"What inspires you, Walter? Where do the ideas for your stories come from?"

Walter frowned, looked at his big hands and gave the matter some thought. "Vince, promise me that you'll never tell anyone."

"I promise," I said, beginning to realize that the list of promises I had to keep was rapidly growing.

"Martha's my inspiration. I wrote my first novel because of her, and every one since then."

"We are talking about *Eddie's wife*?" I replied.

"Of course. I've been in love with Martha for as long as I can recall. We grew up together. My heart was broken when she married Eddie. Eddie's a good man, mind you, but that doesn't change my feelings about Martha."

"Does either Martha or Eddie know?" I asked.

"No, I'm quite sure they don't – and they never will. I would never do anything to hurt either of them. Never."

"Walter, I realize that this is none of my business but wouldn't it be best to try to forget about Martha? Have you considered moving from Avalon and finding someone else? Martha's a fine woman, but I'm sure there must be someone else out there. It's a big world."

"Now, Vince, if I found someone else I couldn't hardly be inspired to write another romance novel, now could I?"

I couldn't argue with that kind of logic.

24
WEDNESDAY, 10 JUNE 1997:
WEDDING PLANS

I heard the throaty roar of Alice's Morgan Plus 8 a little after noon. It had been more than a month since Jenny's funeral and since Bertie and Alice had left for London. It seemed longer. Even with the newfound companionship of Walter, I missed Bertie.

The lovebirds greeted me with ear-to-ear grins. Alice started to say something but Bertie interrupted. He was clearly excited.

"Lo, Vince. As I mentioned on the phone, Alice and I have a surprise." With that, Bertie paused, removed his glasses, and gave me a good look over. "My word," he continued, "you are looking well. Village life seems to suit you."

"Bertie, I feel great. Best I've felt in years. But what's the surprise?"

"Ah, the surprise. Vince, Alice and I are getting married – here in the village, the end of the month."

"That's wonderful," I replied, giving Alice a hug and shaking Bertie's hand. "I'm so happy for both of you."

"Thanks, Vince," said Alice, "but Bertie's only told you half of the story. We'd like for you to be best man." Bertie nodded his approval.

"I'd be delighted. There's nothing more I would like than to serve as best man, for my best friend."

That evening the three of us had dinner at the *Forest City*. None of us, however, indulged in the beer. Instead, Bertie insisted on bringing the jug of homemade rum that Nigel's wife had given him the morning we had left his flat on the quest that had ultimately brought us to Avalon.

Eddie brought a bottle of triple sec, a glass of lime juice, and another glass of pineapple juice to our table, then watched in either admiration or bemusement as Bertie mixed up a concoction he called Barbados Punch. It was, to my taste, just awful. However Bertie and Alice seemed to enjoy it, and who was I to question their choice of a celebratory drink.

At the conclusion of the meal Martha walked to our table and removed her apron. Everyone in the pub suddenly went quiet, turned around in the chairs, and focused their attention on our table.

"Martha has agreed to serenade us," said Bertie, giving me a rather malicious wink. With that, Martha began to sing what had become, for me, a very familiar song – "The White Cliffs of Dover." After the second chorus everyone in the pub joined in.

It was dopey. It was corny. It was wonderful.

25
SATURDAY, 27 JUNE 1997:
THE WEDDING AND A RECEPTION

Alice and Bertie's wedding was simply outstanding. The entire village was in attendance, along with some very special outsiders. Nigel, Abdul and their families were there, along with the Devlin sisters. Best of all, though, was the fact that Hazel, Stanley, and Diana were able to come. Of course, all the "outsiders" were advised not to drink the local water.

Hazel and Diana examined me as thoroughly as one could a fully clothed man. They seemed satisfied that I was doing well, if not in remission. Diana was quite sure it was the Marmite. I couldn't disagree.

Stanley said nothing about my appearance, but did inquire about the Morris Minor. I assured him that I was keeping it in tip-top shape, and promised to give him a ride after the reception.

The reception was held on the grounds of the village schoolhouse. As the best man, I sat at the bride and groom's table, along with the vicar, Martha – the matron of honor – and Eddie. Diana, Stanley and Hazel were seated at an adjoining table, with the members of the village council.

As I gave my toast to the bride and groom I noticed a rather peculiar thing. Bobby Kipling was staring at Diana. In fact, his eyes never left her during the entire toast.

Diana, for her part, seemed unsettled by the attention. Finishing the toast, I nudged Bertie and mentioned that Bobby seemed to have taken quite an interest in Diana.

At the conclusion of the meal, Bertie walked to Diana's table. He whispered something in Diana's ear. Her initial frown turned into a smile, and she turned in her seat and gave Bobby a nod. For the next half-hour or so the two were inseparable, wandering the grounds, conversing, and laughing.

The first opportunity I had to corner Bertie I gave him a questioning look, and then nodded toward Diana and Bobby.

"Bertie, isn't Bobby a married man? What's this thing going on with him and Diana?"

"No worries, Vince. Bobby's happily married. He just thought, however, that he might know Diana from the war. They're simply talking about the old days. War stories I would suppose. Nothing untoward going on."

So Bertie's story was that the two knew each other from the war. My guess was that Bobby Kipling had been the tall, skinny Yank that had hung around outside of the field hospital while Diana cared for his best friend.

After the reception Alice and Bertie left on their honeymoon. It was to last the entire summer, starting in Italy, on to Greece, and from there to New Zealand and the States. For a guy who hadn't wanted to budge from London for thirty years, Bertie had suddenly become the dedicated world traveler.

Amazingly, and touchingly, I received a call from Bertie every evening – no matter where in the world he and Alice might be. He was still checking up on me.

26
SUMMER 1997:
CONSUMED BY CURIOSITY

I spent the summer of 1997 enjoying village life and giving thanks for the respite from the pain that had plagued me for the past two years. I began to attend church, something I had neglected for the past two years, and found Henry Kitcatt to be an unusual and, albeit on rare occasion, riveting speaker. I most enjoyed it, however, when Eddie would stand in for the vicar. It seemed that there was no sermon that didn't include the mention of beer.

Twice a week Walter and I went fishing. For some reason the big fellow felt comfortable confiding in me, possibly because he liked and trusted me, or possibly because he felt that I wouldn't be around that much longer. Whatever the reason, he was good company.

On one of our trips, in late August, Walter seemed in a particularly talkative mood. He had finished the *Tattered Tartan* and was laying out plans for his next novel. This one would take place in Ireland, and he intended to spend the next two months there to obtain, so he claimed, "a feel of the place." He described the outline of the new novel, one that would take place during the famine and the migration of so many Irish from their homeland. He was debating as to whether to title it *The Shattered Shamrock* or *By Way of Cobh*.

I must admit to not really giving Walter my full attention. Despite the fact that I felt well at the time, in two months I might not be here. I had, in fact, already lived beyond the predictions of my physicians. This could well be my last fishing trip with Walter.

While I wasn't too pleased with the thought of dying, I have to admit that I was even more concerned about dying without learning the truth about the *Susan Rae* and its survivors. Bertie might have lost all interest in that matter, and he might have accepted Bobby Kipling's explanation, but I was determined to get some straight answers, even at the risk of incurring the displeasure of my new friend.

"Walter," I said, as he made a perfect cast to a point upstream, "what did you think of those photos? The ones that were on my kitchen table that evening you brought your pies and puddings?"

"What should I think of them?" he answered, his eyes focused upstream.

"Well, they're both supposedly photos of the *Susan Rae*, a B17 Flying Fortress. But one, the picture with the crew standing by the plane, has the name *Susan Rae* painted on the nose. The other, the plane that crash-landed outside of Lower Friththingden, has absolutely nothing painted on its nose. No name, no drawing of a woman, nothing. But they are the same planes … aren't they?"

"Vince, I truly have no idea as to what you're talking about. If you're looking for information on the American B17 crash survivors that were stationed north of here, during the war, you really need to talk to my father," said Walter, making yet another picture-perfect cast. "In fact, I never knew until just now that their plane was named the *Susan Rae*."

"I'm sorry; I just assumed that you were aware of the facts as to the American survivors. But I'm not sure that it would do much good to talk to your dad. From what Bertie tells me your father insists that the five survivors of the *Susan Rae* are all dead."

Walter retrieved his line and turned to me, a puzzled look on his face. "That's right, Vince, they're all dead – every last one of them."

"I'm not sure I believe that," I replied. "What about your father?"

Walter shook his head in disbelief. "Vince, Dad's from Canada. He was an infantryman in the war, with the Canadian Army. Are you actually under the impression that Dad's one of the five Yanks?"

"That's my best guess," I replied.

"Well, Vince, you're dead wrong."

I had the feeling that Walter really believed what he was saying. There seemed to be no point in pressing the matter.

"All right. Sorry to have brought it up," I said. "But there's another matter that I'd like to discuss. What about the so-called pollution in this valley. How did that story get started?"

"Have you been talking to Bertie about the pollution?" asked Walter.

"Bertie won't talk about the pollution. He tells me he's sworn to secrecy. And that, of course, makes it clear that the pollution story is bogus."

"Well, since you've seen through our little fib, I suppose I might as well tell you the whole story," said Walter. "Doug Stevenson and Dad had taken a trip to London, sometime back in the late seventies. On their way back they visited Stratford-on-Avon. Doug loved Shakespeare and wanted to visit the bard's birthplace. What they encountered was traffic jams, hordes of pushy tourists, and lots of souvenir stands – of course it's even worse now. They were both appalled, and decided that they would do whatever it took to avoid having something like that inflicted on Avalon."

"I suppose I can understand their feelings," I said.

Walter nodded, then continued. "They decided that a polluted village, or at least one that people thought was polluted, would be safe from an invasion of tourists. The pair managed to get some soil that had been polluted by chemicals at a petrochemical plant. They brought it back to Avalon in a plastic bag. Then they asked Richard, Alice's late husband, to test the soil. They told Richard that the sample had come from the headwaters of our local river."

"So neither Richard nor Alice knew that the pollution story was bogus?" I asked.

"That's right. They had no reason to believe that Doug and Dad were lying to them. In fact, until a few weeks ago, only the five of us on the parish council knew the truth about the 'pollution.' Now, of course, you and Bertie know that there's no pollution here. So that makes seven."

"So Bertie knows that the pollution matter is a sham. Yet he's moved to Waddington in order to maintain that story," I remarked.

"Yes, that was a bit of a tricky matter. If he had just moved into the village, and nothing happened to his health, we would have been found out," said Walter.

"But now that poor man is forced to live in Waddington, while his wife lives in Avalon. All for the sake of keeping up a lie," I replied.

"The council believes that they have found a way around that. Unfortunately, it involves yet another fabrication. We're going to tell everyone that Bertie's been immunized against the effects of the pollution. Bertie, as you probably know, is quite a wealthy chap. Made lots of money in real estate investments. So we decided that we would tell everyone that he paid some enormous amount of money to be immunized. We were planning on doing that this fall, when Bertie and Alice return from their honeymoon, and then Bertie can stay in Avalon."

"Walter, these are all good intentions. But I have to say that they are built on a foundation of lies and deceit. I just hope that everything doesn't fall apart."

"You and me both, Vince. I have to admit that one lie does lead to another. However, the council is hoping that this will be the end of it. We'll do everything we can to protect Avalon, but we're agreed that the fabrications have to end."

I wondered if Walter, a man writing romance novels under a woman's name, might not find that an ironic statement. However, I simply nodded my head.

"Vince," said Walter, "Everything I've told you today is to remain confidential. This is between you and me."

"I understand," I replied.

27
FALL 1997:
THE FOUNDATION

Bertie and Alice returned to Avalon in September, bubbling over with tales to tell, along with what appeared to be at least a thousand photographs of birds. Bertie, in particular, seemed enthralled with travel, and was already planning their next trip.

Just as Walter had predicted, Bertie moved out of his rented house in Waddington and into Alice's cottage. The villagers – or at least most of them – were amazed that Bertie loved Alice so much that he had spent a fortune on being immunized against the valley's "deadly pollution."

They were even more amazed when it was announced that Bertie had established a private "foundation," one that would provide the funds necessary to immunize others who wished to live in Avalon. Of course, as Bertie claimed – and the council agreed, the costs of such immunizations were such that they could be provided to only a small, select group of people. As such, it wasn't a huge surprise that the first recipient of the foundations largess was the husband of Alice's daughter. If liars could ever be made saints, I'd say that Bertie was in line for Sainthood.

My health continued to improve, something I attributed to the fact that I now seemed surrounded by people who seemed to truly care for me. Of course, just to make sure, I continued the daily doses of Marmite.

My monthly meetings with Bobby Kipling centered mostly on the Cleveland Indians. If he knew that I knew who he really was, he never let on.

When I happened to ask Walter Kipling about the stories of his father's failing health, he explained that hadn't "exactly" been a lie. Bobby Kipling and Doug Stevenson had been very close, and the death of Doug had been a terrible shock to Bobby. Bobby had fallen into a depression, leaving the villagers the impression that his problems were physical, rather than emotional.

Bobby had finally faced up to the fact that he would never again see his closest friend and had fallen back into his daily routine of overseeing his surprisingly far-flung brewery operations. That business, Walter informed me, was one of the reasons for the valley's financial well-being. Not only was it a source of employment, but also most of the profits were donated to the village, for distribution by the parish council.

#####

Whenever he and Alice were not travelling, Bertie joined Walter and me on our fishing sojourns. Bertie never picked up a fishing rod, but used the trips to pursue his birding passion. When he took a break from his birding the three of us would sit on the river's bank and discuss the latest village doings and gossip. Never once, however, was the subject of the *Susan Rae*, or the valley's pollution, ever brought up.

When not fishing, or at the *Forest City*, or visiting with Bertie and Alice, I spent my time either gardening or cooking – two hobbies that I had never engaged in until my arrival in Avalon. And, whenever time permitted, I'd read one in the long series of Catherine Clovelly's romance novels.

Although I can't say that I ever became a romance novel fan, I did find the books revealing. I soon came to realize that, in every one of the books, the heroine and hero were thinly veiled versions of Martha and Walter. Whether the story took place in England, Scotland, Ireland, or New Zealand, and regardless of the names of the heroine or hero, it was Martha who ultimately ended up in the arms of Walter.

28
SPRING 1998:
ZERO TO SIXTY IN UNDER SEVEN SECONDS

When spring returned to Avalon I was more than a little surprised to find myself still above ground. I would guess that a few of the villagers shared my sense of wonder. I wasn't sure if it was the Marmite, the "polluted" water, or the local beer, but I felt splendid.

The improvement in my physical condition had not escaped Bertie's notice. He recommended that we celebrate my good health with something special and suggested a road trip – one that was to include a visit to Stanley and Hazel at their cottage in Kent. It sounded like a fine plan, and I suggested that we take the Morris Minor. I even offered to let him drive. Bertie, however, had other ideas.

"Vince," Bertie said disapprovingly, "I dearly love the old Morris but, to be honest, I've found that a trip in any motorcar that can't do at least 100 mph gives me a headache. Did you know that Alice's Morgan Plus 8 can do 124 mph, and has a 0 to 60 time of less than seven seconds? It's lovely to cruise along, top down, wind in your hair, knowing that you can pass almost every other motorcar on the road. I tell you, Vince, you haven't experienced true motoring until you've ridden in a Plus 8."

I was tempted to ask how the Morgan's gas mileage compared to the Morris Minor, but decided to let the matter drop. So it was that the two of us started our journey in a cherry red Morgan Plus 8, our luggage strapped onto a rack mounted on the rear of the car.

Walter and Alice waved us goodbye as Bertie drove through the village – at a crawl.

"Alice insists that I keep the motorcar under 10 mph until we're out of sight of the village," he explained.

Once we reached the main road Bertie floored the accelerator pedal. In no time the speedometer on the Plus 8 was registering over 100 mph – and my pulse rate was about fifty points higher.

"Bertie, perhaps you'd better slow down a bit. If you get a ticket at this speed they may just take away your license."

Bertie shot me a sideways glance, grinning like the proverbial Cheshire cat. "No worries, Vince, I haven't as yet had time to get a license."

I suppose there may have been some logic to that reply but, if so, it escaped me. I gave up trying to slow Bertie down. While he assiduously obeyed the speed limits through the towns and villages, the second he reached an open stretch of highway we were off like a bullet.

"Bertie, did you always drive this damn fast? Is this the way you drove before the accident with the lorry?"

"Oh no. I doubt if I ever drove faster than fifty. Mum would have had a fit. But then, things have changed, wouldn't you say?"

I had to agree. "Things" had definitely changed over the course of the past year. Bertie had certainly changed and, as I reflected on the matter, so had I. The anger and bitterness that had consumed me for years seemed to have dissipated. Even at that very moment, racing along at breakneck speed, when a part of me feared for my very life, I found that I was actually enjoying myself.

Not only had I changed but also England itself seemed to have changed over the course of the past year. The countryside seemed lovelier, its people more agreeable. Bertie, however, seemed to disagree with my assessment.

"The people haven't changed," he said. "It's *you* who has changed."

We arrived at Stanley and Hazel's cottage at about five that evening, having averaged – according to Bertie's calculations – a brilliant 71.3 mph for the trip, our leisurely lunch break not included. We were greeted like family members – well-loved family members – and spent the evening catching up on the events of the past year.

Stanley, we discovered, had taken up painting. His specialty was watercolors of doors and entranceways. After spending fifty years as a doorman, I would have thought that a door was the last thing he would want to paint. The paintings were, however, quite charming.

Bertie and I were each made a gift of a painting. Bertie's was of the remarkably short door of a restaurant in Bradford-on-Avon. Mine was, in my mind, even more special. Stanley had painted the door of my cottage in Avalon, from memory.

The next morning Stanley prepared us all a full English breakfast. We were then taken for a morning drive, in the blue Rover, around and about the area. I would imagine that, at one time, it was quite beautiful. Unfortunately, where I was informed that there had once been fields of hops and grains, and acre upon acre of orchards, the land was now mostly housing developments – exceptionally expensive houses set on remarkably small tracts of land.

After lunch at Stanley and Hazel's favorite restaurant we bid the old couple goodbye – and promised to visit again … soon. Once we were on the motorway Bertie volunteered his opinion as to the area.

"Vince, this region was once known as the garden of England. It's still quite lovely but, based on the new houses, businesses, and traffic that we've encountered, I'd say that England is on the verge of losing its garden."

"I suppose," I replied, "that not every place is so fortunate as to have Avalon's pollution."

Bertie refused to take the bait. "No, I suppose not. Our pollution problem does have a way of stopping 'progress' in its tracks, doesn't it?"

"Yes, that it does." Changing the subject, I added, "Now let's see how fast this little red machine can go, Bertie. Tonight's Jugged Hare night at the *Forest City*."

29
SUNDAY, 26 APRIL 1998:
JENNY'S BIRTHDAY SURPRISE

I rolled over in bed, turned on the light, and checked the clock on the nightstand. It was a little after five in the morning. I gave up on any idea of going back to sleep and decided to get an early start on the day.

It wasn't until I had finished brushing my teeth that I realized what day it was. It was 26 April, Jenny's birthday – her fifty-second birthday.

I finished dressing and strolled to the rear garden, where I picked a dozen red roses. By then the sun had risen, and I took the well-worn path leading from my garden to the village churchyard. The morning was chilly, and a gentle breeze rustled the tender new leaves on the trees along the pathway.

As I approached the churchyard I realized that I wasn't the only one up early. Bobby Kipling was in the yard, his back to me. My first thought was that he was visiting the grave of his friend, Doug Stevenson, and that it was a rather odd time to do so. But, as I got closer I realized that Bobby was standing next to Jenny's grave.

I didn't quite know what to make of it and decided to stop and watch. From my vantage point I could see Bobby's profile quite clearly. His eyes were closed but his mouth was moving. It appeared that Bobby was praying.

Just then the wind picked up. A sudden gust lifted Bobby's long hair just enough for me to get a quick glimpse of the left side of his head. It was exactly what I expected. The man most definitely was absent his left ear.

Bobby opened his eyes and turned. It was evident that he was surprised to see me – possibly as surprised as I was to find him beside Jenny's grave.

"Good morning, Vince. I see that you've brought roses for Jenny. You'd best weigh them down with a rock. In this breeze they'll be gone before you know it."

"Good morning, Bobby. It's just now sunrise and you've already given me two surprises."

"Two surprises?" said Bobby. "I suppose that one would be seeing me at Jenny's grave. What would the other be?"

"Actually, the other isn't that much of a surprise – it's what I've suspected for almost a year. Bobby, you swore to Bertie that the five Americans were long dead. But that was a lie, wasn't it? You're the survivor of the *Susan Rae* who lost his left ear. Don't try to tell me otherwise."

"What I told Bertie was that the *Americans* he was looking for are all dead. That, Vince, I can swear to. What I didn't tell Bertie was that two of the crew of the *Susan Rae* were *Canadian* citizens – that would be myself and Doug Stevenson."

"What would two Canadians be doing in an American B17?" I asked.

"Doug and I were from the same little town in Canada, St. Catharines. Back then his name was Doug White; mine was Bobby Dombrowski. Doug went to the States to attend college – to Miami University in Oxford, Ohio to be exact. When he finished there he took a teaching job in New York State, and filled out the paperwork to become a U.S. citizen. When I was ready to attend college, Doug recommended that I enroll at Miami University. That's where I was when the war began. That's when Doug and I enlisted – with a little help from one of Doug's influential friends – in the American Army Air Corps. Vince, even though we were on an American plane, in American uniforms, we were still – technically at least – Canadian citizens. So, when Bertie asked me about the

American survivors of the *Susan Rae*, I told him the truth – they were long dead. He never asked me about any Canadian survivors."

"Okay, you didn't lie – but you certainly evaded the truth. Now, how about explaining your early morning visit to my wife's grave?"

Bobby looked skyward, sighed, and then answered. "It's Jenny's birthday. It's my daughter's birthday. That's why I'm here."

"Jenny? Your daughter? What the hell are you talking about?" I said, my mind trying desperately to grasp the situation.

"Vince, it's a long story – and not one that I'm particularly proud of. But I suppose it's one that you deserve to hear."

"You're damn right, and I'd like to hear it right now," I replied.

Bobby averted his eyes and then began his story. "It was the summer of 1945. Doug had managed, just a few months earlier, to convince the British government to allow the villagers to return to Avalon or, as it was known then, as Withington-in-the-Marsh. There were a lot of single women and widows in that group. There were, in particular, two very attractive sisters: Eve and Emma Bartlett. Eve was twenty-one; Emma was seventeen. Eve was cool and aloof. Emma was the talkative and outgoing one. They were both beautiful. I was pretty full of myself back then and I immediately made it clear that I was interested in both of them. Eve played hard to get, but it was obvious that Emma had a crush on me. So, fool that I was, I decided to lead Emma on, hoping that this would make Eve jealous."

Bobby paused, sighed, and then continued. "Emma loved to paint. She particularly enjoyed painting this little church behind me. That summer she sketched the church from every angle possible, and then finally began to paint it from across the brook. There are trees between the church and that site now, but back then you had a clear view of the church. She and I would meet over there, and I'd watch her paint – and tell her how much I cared for her. But all the while, I was falling harder and harder for her sister."

"Bobby, are you trying to tell me that this Emma person, Emma Bartlett, was Jenny's mother?" I asked.

"That's exactly what I'm trying to say. The attention I gave Emma did exactly what I hoped for – it made Eve jealous. Three months later Eve and I announced our engagement. The very next day Emma vanished. She just disappeared without trace. No note, no final farewell. Vince, I honestly didn't know what happened to her until Bertie showed me the copy of the painting by Jenny's mother. I knew as soon as I laid eyes on that print that it was Emma's work. I asked Bertie if he knew who painted it. He told me that a woman named Emma Ambrose was the artist, and that she was Jenny's mother. He told me that Emma Ambrose had married his uncle and, after his uncle died, she and her daughter – Jenny – had moved to the States. I finally got up the courage to ask him about Jenny's date of birth and death – pretending that I needed it for the parish records. As you well know, Jenny was born on 26 April 1946. Vince, that was just six months after Emma disappeared. I realized at that moment that you and Bertie were asking for permission to bury the ashes of my own daughter in the very same village where she was conceived." Bobby started to say something more, but his eyes filled with tears and he looked away.

"My God," I said. "My God."

"Vince, why don't we walk back to your cottage? There's more I need to tell you. Much more."

#####

Neither of us spoke on the walk back to the cottage. I simply had nothing to say. I prepared tea for the both of us and asked Bobby if he'd care for breakfast.

"Not now, Vince. But maybe after I get a few things more off my chest."

I sat down at the table, across from Bobby, and waited to hear the rest of his story.

"Vince, just as you suspected, I survived the crash-landing of the *Susan Rae*."

"In Lower Friththingden? On 22 December 1943?"

"That's right," said Bobby. "The *Susan Rae* was badly shot up. Most of the instruments were either not working or malfunctioning. Doug, our pilot, had no idea as to his altitude. Suddenly, however, we broke through the cloud cover – just a few hundred feet above the village of Lower Friththingden. Doug pulled back on the yoke, trying to gain altitude, but the plane was nearly out of fuel. He managed to gain a few hundred feet, saw a clearing to the north of the village, and headed for it. That's when we ran into something."

"You ran into something? The land around Lower Friththingden is flat as a pancake. What on earth did you run into?" I asked.

"Nothing on earth, Vince. Our starboard wing hooked a descending parachute. Attached to the parachute was a German mine – a one-thousand pounder. When Doug saw that he dipped the wing, and the parachute slid off. According to what he was told later, the mine landed on the village pub."

"Right, it landed on the *Sow and Centipede*. Ah, so that's how the pub was destroyed."

"That's right. Luckily no one was in the pub at the time. Doug, me and the three other survivors were taken to a farmhouse near the landing. A few minutes later two Rolls-Royces roared into the back garden of the farmhouse. The occupants of the cars treated us like heroes. Doug couldn't figure it out until one of the group, a civilian in an expensive Bond Street suit, thanked him for saving the villagers by 'selflessly risking his own life and hooking the parachute mine.' Doug had to struggle to keep from laughing. It had been nothing but pure chance that had saved the villagers.

Luckily, we all kept our mouths shut. The civilian informed Doug that he and the rest of the crew could have anything they wanted. A grateful British Government, so the fellow said, was prepared to grant our every wish. Doug huddled with us and then told the civilian that all that we wanted was to be out of the war. We'd had quite enough, thank you. The civilian blinked and said something about getting approval. He went outside, to one of the cars, and spoke to someone in it."

"Winston Churchill?" I asked.

"We weren't sure who it was; all we knew was that it must have been someone very important. The civilian returned a few minutes later, called Doug aside, and told him that it had been taken care of. Within the hour we were loaded into a lorry and ultimately arrived at the military installation just northwest of here. The barracks we were housed in are gone now – as you already know – but we stayed there until the spring of 1944. By then we were having second thoughts about our decision. We felt guilty about sitting out the war while a lot of good men were out there still fighting. Doug told our contact in the government that we had changed our minds; that we wanted back in the war. The contact informed Doug that, if that was what we really wanted, it would be arranged. Of course, since we were officially declared dead – and had promised to never return to the States or reveal the agreement we had reached with the British government – we would have to join up with a Canadian regiment. That's how the five of us wound up as infantrymen in the Canadian Army."

"And that's how the other crewmembers died?"

"That's right, only Doug and I survived the war. The others, the American crewmembers, were killed in action. Somehow Doug and I managed to get through the rest of the war without a scratch."

"Okay, but there's another thing that's always bothered me. What happened to the nose art on the plane that crash-landed? I have a photo of the crew standing in front of the

Susan Rae and in that photo the name and a sketch of a blonde woman are on the nose. But the plane that crash-landed had no nose art whatsoever."

"Walter told me that you were asking about that. Walter, by the way, knows nothing about what I've been telling you. The answer to the nose art question is not that complicated, although it did make Doug mad every time he talked about it. Doug named our B17 after his very pretty young wife, Susan Rae White. Unfortunately, Susan Rae was quite the loose woman. She repeatedly cheated on Doug, but he kept forgiving her and taking her back – at least until a few days before the last flight of the *Susan Rae*. Doug was informed that his wife was pregnant, and that the father was their next-door neighbor back in New York State. That very night he helped the ground crew paint over her name and sketch on the nose of the plane. Of course, I guess that little tragedy made it even easier for him to fall head over heels in love with your friend, Diana."

"Doug was in love with Diana Brooks? Are you sure?" I asked.

"Absolutely sure. Doug fell in love with Diana during the time she was caring for him – when he and the rest of us were stationed northwest of here. Doug told her that he was mad about her, but Diana didn't take him seriously. She told him that every soldier she had ever tended to had claimed to want to marry her – and that they all went back to their wives or girl friends once they were well. But Doug never forgot Diana – and, in my opinion, wasted his life mooning over a woman he couldn't have."

Much like someone else we both know, I thought.

"Anyhow, once the war ended Doug and I decided to return to this valley and, as Doug said, breathe life back into it. And he did, in my opinion, a damn fine job of it."

Bobby Kipling paused and stared at his empty cup of tea. I asked him if he wanted a refill, but he seemed not to hear me.

"There's something else you should know," said Bobby. "We're visited once a year by a 'minder,' a civil servant who is tasked with checking up on us."

"You get checked out once a year? What exactly does this civil servant look for?" I asked.

"He wants to make sure that I'm keeping my mouth shut. It would be a major embarrassment to the British government if it ever got out that they were involved in covering up the disappearance of an American aircraft and its crew. He also checks to see if at least one of the survivors of the *Susan Rae*, or at least one of his direct descendants, still lives in the valley."

"Why's that?"

"It was part of the agreement. The British government agreed to let the survivors of the *Susan Rae* opt out of the war – and to settle in Avalon – and pretty much do as we pleased with the village and valley. But some bureaucrat slipped in the requirement that the agreement would remain in force only if at least one survivor, or one of his direct descendants, was living here. In the event that part of the agreement is not fulfilled, the entire area reverts back to the British Army – and the villagers will be required to leave."

"My God," I said. "Your son is the last direct descendant."

"That's right. The future of Avalon, and this valley, rests in the awkward hands of Walter Kipling."

30
WINTER 2003:
SIX AND A HALF YEARS

As I look back on the past six and a half years I can't help but marvel at the changes in my life. Bertie remains my dearest friend, although it's a close race between him and Walter. Two years after arriving in Avalon, and once the parish council decided that I might actually be around for a while, I was offered the job of school headmaster.

I informed them that I would accept the position only if I could have Wednesdays off – one of the two days a week that Walter and I go fishing. They agreed and I began my second academic career, although I must admit that I had not looked forward to it. I accepted the position only because I felt that I owed the villagers, and particularly the members of the council. It was not long before I fell in love with the job and, most of all, the children.

I offered to pay a more reasonable rent on the cottage and Bobby Kipling took me up on it. In 1999 my rent was doubled, from one to two pounds. Bobby assured me that he just might double it again, in five years. I jokingly suggested that, since he was in essence my father-in-law, a one hundred percent increase in my rent seemed a bit harsh.

On 10 June 2000 I once again served as best man for an Avalon wedding. Walter Kipling married his literary agent, a woman that looked remarkably – and disturbingly – enough like Martha to have been her younger sister. That happy event ended the Catherine Clovelly romance books and resulted in the loss of both of their jobs. A year later Walter became a new father and the future of Avalon seemed assured, for at least another generation.

As I reflect on the past six years I believe that I've finally come to understand and even forgive myself. I realize now that it wasn't England that I had detested for so many years; it was my fear of England. I wanted Jenny to myself, and saw England – and her countrymen – as challengers for her affection. From there it wasn't much of a leap to blame England for her death. Jenny had, after all, returned from her last visit to her homeland with pneumonia. While she recovered from that, her already frail health was broken. Jenny spent the final years of her life as an invalid. I needed someone to blame for her illness and demise. England and the English were convenient and easy targets.

My own health has been, for the most part, excellent. I must admit, however, that shortly after my sixtieth birthday, a few months ago, I have begun to feel my age. I suppose that is to be expected. While I'm well and happy, there's something that I've missed. It's been more than six years since Bertie and I took that fateful trip from London to Avalon. Since then I've only driven the Morris Minor to and from Waddington, and that no more than once or twice a month. Bertie and Alice will be back from Peru in late December, and I've decided to ask him to join me on one more excursion on his return – in the Morris Minor rather than his Plus 8. The Morris Minor has been serviced and polished – with Walter's help – to a fine sheen. I look forward to Bertie's return.

EPILOGUE
BY ALBERT "BERTIE" AMBROSE, III

Vince Collesano passed away on the 10th of January 2004. Per the instructions he had given the vicar some two weeks earlier, his death was listed as having been caused by the "deadly pollution that had so despoiled Avalon and the valley surrounding it." It was the last of his many gifts to the community he had grown to love.

Vince's funeral was held three days later and was attended by everyone in the village, as well as two dear friends from elsewhere in England. Using the names that Vince assigned to them in the manuscript for this book, those "outsiders" were Stanley and Hazel. I'm sure that had Diana lived, she too would have attended. However that lovely lady died, at age ninety, only a few days prior to Vince's passing.

Vicar Henry Kitcatt conducted the funeral. I – the chap identified as "Bertie" in the manuscript – read the eulogy, just as I had at Jenny's funeral some six years earlier. As Vince's casket was lowered into his final resting place, Martha sang what had over the past six years become his favorite song, "The White Cliffs of Dover."

It was quite possible that Walter, Bobby and I were the only ones who saw the irony in that selection. The song, as was mentioned early on in Vince's story, was inspired by the poem written by Alice Duer Miller, an American. Another American – one who had never even visited England, composed the song itself. And the song was sung at the funeral of a man who had once detested England and all it stands for – or at least that's what Vince had once believed.

When Alice and I returned to Avalon, Christmas 2003, we were met by a Vince Collesano who seemed to have aged at least twenty years since our last meeting just three months earlier. Vince hugged us, and then asked if he might talk to me in private. The two of us walked outside, into the well cared for and much loved back garden of his cottage. It was there that Vince made his final request of me. He asked that the two of us take, for old time's sake, one more trip in the Morris Minor. He insisted that I drive.

We left for Port Isaac on Friday evening, the 9th of January and rented rooms at a hotel on the hill above the village. The next morning I drove to the cliffs above the town and we took a brief stroll along the path that lay next to the cliffs. It was cold and windy, but that didn't seem to bother Vince. His only remarks were that he only wished that he had been able to visit the spot with Jenny.

Looking tired and worn, Vince suggested that we return to the motorcar. I helped him into the ancient vehicle and took my seat on the driver's side. I turned to speak to Vince, to ask him where to next, when he put his hand on mine.

"Bertie, let's go home." Those were his last words.

THE END.

ABOUT THE AUTHOR

James Ignizio received a Ph.D. in Engineering from Virginia Tech in 1971. He is a Fellow of the Institute of Industrial Engineering, a Fellow of the British Operational Research Society, a Fellow of the World Academy of Productivity Sciences, and recipient of the First Hartford Prize. He began his professional career as an engineer on the Saturn/Apollo manned moon-landing mission.

Ignizio is the author of ten books and more than 360 publications, including over 150 peer reviewed papers in international professional journals. After spending the better part of three decades as a university professor, he has escaped the strange and quirky world of academia to fulfill a life-long desire to write something other than textbooks and technical papers. *The Last English Village* is his first novel.

17517671R00131

Made in the USA
San Bernardino, CA
12 December 2014